A Charm of Powerful Trouble

A Charm of Powerful Trouble

JOANNE HORNIMAN

ALLEN&UNWIN

Allen & Unwin
83 Alexander St
Crows Nest NSW 2065
Australia
Phone: (61 2) 8425 0100
Fax: (61 2) 9906 2218
Email: info@allenandunwin.com
Web: www.allenandunwin.com

National Library of Australia
Cataloguing-in-Publication entry:

Horniman, Joanne.
A charm of powerful trouble.

ISBN 1 86508 837 4.

1. Mothers and daughters – New South Wales – Fiction.
2. Sisters – New South Wales – Fiction. I. Title.

A823.3

Designed by Jo Hunt
Set in 11 on 15 pt Berkeley Book by Midland Typesetters
Printed by McPherson's Printing Group

10 9 8 7 6 5 4 3 2 1

For my family and friends

Acknowledgements

I'd like to warmly thank the following people: Margaret Connolly, Erica Wagner and Sarah Brenan for their support and enthusiasm; Faye Bolton and Pip Davenport for showing me microscopes; Scot Gardner for generously giving me butterflies; my sister Joyce for introducing me to Christina Rossetti at such an early age; Jacqui Kent for sending a title my way (which is, of course, by William Shakespeare). And Tony Chinnery, as always, for everything.

Contents

The Aubergines

CHILDREN KNOW when there are secrets.

The house where I grew up reeked of them. Secrets had been layered into the mud-brick walls that my mother and father had built, and secrets fluttered with the tiny bats that lived under the eaves and found their way inside each evening to dance under the cavernous ceiling. Secrets shone from the ferocious red of the hibiscus flowers in the garden, and they rotted with the leaves that lay on the rainforest floor.

In that place, my sister and I lived a charmed life.

For a long time I didn't distinguish between myself and Lizzie. We were Lizzie–Laura or Laura–Lizzie, part of a single consciousness. Our lives were full of exhilaration and endless play. We ate when we were hungry, slept when we were tired, and woke the next morning to more sunlight or to rain, to a garden full of light and shadow and the cries of birds. We made tunnels through the undergrowth to find bowerbird nests, and built towns from sticks and palm fronds. Our parents drove us to the beach, and the car swooped down the mountain through tunnels of green. We came home with our skin salty and the cracks in our fannies filled with sand.

And all through our childhood, Lizzie sang. She sang as she squatted on the ground arranging sticks into houses and streets; she sang as she built sandcastles and decorated them with shells and stones and seaweed, and she sang as she walked with a bent back through the lantana on one of our expeditions. It was a soft, melodious song, a kind of hum, and she made it up as she went along. I identified myself with Lizzie so much that I imagined I also sang. It wasn't until years later, when she stopped singing, that I realised I couldn't.

We went to school, but that was a nuisance and an inter-ruption. I made no real friends. Lizzie, just two years older, was enough for me. I don't think I even bothered looking in a mirror till I was ten, and it was then that I realised I wasn't Lizzie, who was tall and blonde and beautiful. Laura, I saw, was brown and stocky and covered with scratches. Of course I'd seen my dark, tangled curls when my mother cut my hair, but I hadn't really believed in them. We had a little sister called Chloe, six years younger than I; we loved her to bits, but she was never one of us, part of Lizzie–Laura.

Our parents were Claudio and Emma: we had been brought up to call them by their first names. We lived on a wild property in the hills behind Mullumbimby. Emma painted pictures and Claudio made documentary films. Claudio was expansive and gregarious; he wanted more and more of life all the time. His laughter seemed to fill the house even when he wasn't there. And he often wasn't there. He was away making films, or sometimes, I now see, simply adventuring. It was our mother who kept us together. Our home was her nest, her retreat, her sanctuary; her studio was an old shed hidden by trees, secretive, like her nature.

My mother loved my father too much. She loved us all too much. It was her weak point, her tender vulnerability. Her strength was in her secrets. Lizzie and I lusted after them; we longed to get inside her head, but lovingly, steadfastly, she kept herself intact from us. We could only wonder.

When I was twelve, we'd lie on the bed together, our legs intertwined, and talk all afternoon. We'd pass food into each other's mouths like a mother bird with her young. That didn't seem revolting to us, but natural, part of our intimacy. For a while it seemed that there was nothing we couldn't say to each other.

On one of those afternoons Lizzie told me that she knew Claudio wasn't her real father. No one had told her, but when she voiced it I saw that I had known all along. It wasn't simply that she looked like a cuckoo child, tall and blonde and pale. It was evident that Claudio didn't really like her. He preferred me and Chloe, dark-haired, dark-eyed

5

copies of himself. There was something in the way he looked at her, detached, without love. He was outwardly magnanimous, but it was beyond his capacity to love a child who wasn't his own.

Lizzie and I would lie in the grass and speculate about what had happened to her real father.

'Killed . . .' we'd say, testing out the idea.

'Gone to America . . .'

'Died young of a dreadful disease . . .'

Our mother had had other people disappear from her life. There was her father, lost in the bush when our mother was only two, his body never found. And her sister Beth had drowned in the ocean at the age of nineteen. It seemed to us that the world had simply swallowed them up. Perhaps it had swallowed Lizzie's father as well.

Our mother never spoke much about her sister; we gleaned only fragments. For the rest we had to imagine her. We'd lie, staring at the clouds, dreaming of our Aunt Beth, who never really got to be our aunt as she died before we were born. In our minds, she was beautiful and clever and funny. She liked pop music and adored the Beatles, especially Paul. But our strongest image of her was in death.

'Drowned . . .' we'd murmur, imagining her floating tidily on an aqua sea, her long hair spread out on the water, hands clasped over her breasts, flowers unaccountably drifting beside her on the swell of the waves.

❧

At twelve I had developed an antenna for the darker side of life, and an interest in it. I assumed there were many layers to people.

That summer Stella and Paris came to visit, driving all the way up from Sydney, and we trooped out of the house to welcome them. Stella was someone our mother knew from her childhood, but this was the first time we'd met her.

She was younger than my mother, tougher, thinner, with a sort of wiry resilience in her body and a childish, unblemished face framed by blonde curls. She was someone who clearly wasn't impressed by children. When she was introduced to us she said 'Hi', then lit a cigarette and gave us a dismissive glance.

Her daughter Paris was ten. She acknowledged us with her eyes but remained silent. Spiky black hair accentuated her pointed, severe little face. I felt that we would stand there forever beside Stella's battered old yellow Corona with Claudio eating Stella up with his eyes. Chloe, who was uncomplicated and plump and calm, stood dreamily humming a tune. Emma hugged Paris, who scowled ungratefully up at her. And Lizzie and I hovered at the edge of the group, Lizzie drawing circles in the dust with her foot.

Three black cockatoos came swooping in with metallic, rolling cries. We lifted our eyes to the sky as they circled above us and watched as they came to rest in a tree next to the house and began to rip away the bark with their beaks, looking for grubs. My mother walked over and flapped her arms at them. 'Shoo!' she called, 'Shoo!' Her movement broke our inertia, and we made our way into the house.

&

At night our house was filled with light and was like a beacon in the dark. I liked it best then, with the dank odour of the forest invading it. In the day, you could see the thin line of the ocean in the distance and I always fancied I could catch a whiff of the sea on the evening air.

That night I stood in the doorway where I could see both inside and outside the house. If I turned my head one way I could see the darkness and imagine everything that was in it. By turning my head the other way, I could see inside the house. It was as high as a church, with a six-metre tree trunk reaching to the ceiling. Tiny bats flew in the high loft windows and out again. These bats were as small as mice; they reminded me of mice, the way they colonised the house. I stood in the doorway and watched the people inside. They thought I was simply dreaming there, my head full of fuzzy twelve-year-old's fantasies.

I watched Claudio and Emma as they lounged on a sofa talking to Stella. They were drinking wine and there was a lot of laughter, but it seemed uneasy to me.

Lizzie sat in a corner and played her electric guitar without the amp. She played the same riff over and over, frowning and biting her bottom lip when she played a wrong note. Lizzie had got the guitar a couple of years before, and now it was her constant companion. She was mad about the guitar – it was her passion; she'd stopped singing when she found the music she could make with it.

Chloe and Paris sat at the dining table, which was still littered with the remains of dinner. They painted a wallaby skull green and orange with model paints, and planned to put candles in the eye sockets when it was finished. Paris rarely smiled, and when she did it was as if something painful was being drawn out of her. Already I knew I didn't like her.

But it was the adults I was interested in. They were saying things that would be worth listening to.

'So,' said Claudio to Emma. 'Tell us about the Aubergines.' He said it lazily, leaning back in the chair, smiling, watching her, but keeping his eye on Stella, too.

Emma shook her head and laughed. It was a regretful, wise laugh, a laugh that remembered things. 'The Aubergines,' she said. 'I'd almost forgotten about the Aubergines.'

'What aubergines?' said Stella.

I saw a familiar flicker in my mother's eyes and I crept over and sat on the floor at my father's feet, watching her.

'Oh God, the Aubergines! They were just a story I used to tell. A true story. About this amazing family I knew when I was young . . .' Emma spoke into the air, looking into the past, seeing herself all those years ago.

'Their name wasn't really Aubergine; they had another name, an Italian name that sounded a bit like aubergine . . . it was Claudio who started calling them the Aubergines.'

'And when we were students, whenever we got bored,'

drawled Claudio, 'which was quite often, sitting around in dark, damp old houses with no money – Emma would amuse us by telling us about the Aubergines.'

'You've never told *us* about these Aubergines,' I said.

'But they were nothing. They weren't important. Just a thing from my childhood. Just a story to amuse people.'

'What were they like?'

'Oh, they were wonderful and awful at the same time.' Emma stared into the shadows of the ceiling. 'They had a wonderful big old house. And it was full of books, and they were always reading them. I could never get enough books. We had hardly any. The Aubergines argued about the books with each other, about what they thought of them, and got quite angry, and thumped tables. Once, Mrs Aubergine *burnt* a book, right at the dining table, with one of the Aubergine children sobbing and trying to stop her. She said the book was *puerile*. I had to go home and look the word up in the dictionary.'

'What else did they do?'

'The parents used to argue a lot, in front of everyone. And once, one of the children said to them scornfully, "Why don't you just get a *divorce*?" That shocked me. I didn't know of anyone who'd been divorced, and here was a child telling his parents to get one.

'And oh – I've forgotten the rest – they don't seem nearly so interesting now.' Emma shook her head and gazed at the floor.

'The children had strange names,' said Claudio. 'Sappho and – what were the others?'

'Sappho and William Carlos Williams and Blake Yeats. Those were the three children. Sappho was my friend from school; that's how I knew the family.'

I kept quizzing her.

'William something Williams? That was a *first* name?'

'Yes. After an American poet that Mrs Aubergine admired. His name was William Carlos Williams Aubergine . . .'

'Except that Aubergine was really an Italian name . . .'

'Yes.'

'And . . . what was the other one's name again?'

'Blake Yeats.' She said it quickly, looking away from me.

'The Aubergines,' said Stella. 'Then you could be the Zucchinis. Zambelli – Zucchini.' She looked at Claudio, whose name it was, and he gave her one of those smiles of his, intense and fleeting and flirtatious, with one eyebrow raised. His eyebrows were astonishing and absurd, but that look could make the person receiving it feel that she was the only one in the world.

My mother laughed uncomfortably. 'The Zucchinis . . . I suppose we could be.'

I settled back against Claudio's knee and he stroked my hair, smoothing down my curls with his square hand. I leaned into him; I knew I was his favourite, I looked so like him. I had his prominent chin and long nose and dark eyes. In the mirror I would practise making my eyes wild with enthusiasm like his when he talked about something that interested him.

I thought about the Aubergines, the story my mother had

11

told, which wasn't much of a story, it was more an evasion of a story. It was all very well talking about these strange Aubergine people, but what was my mother really like in those days? I felt that the story of the Aubergines concealed more than it told.

Lizzie came up, her guitar slung round her neck. 'Mum . . . what's this?' She played a few chords. Lizzie was always asking people if they could recognise the tune she was playing.

'Oh, heavens,' said Emma. 'Play it again . . . "All Along the Watchtower"? No . . . is it "Hey Joe"?'

'No,' said Lizzie. Her face had a stricken expression. 'It was "Purple Haze".'

'Of course. I knew it was something by Jimi Hendrix.'

Lizzie never asked Claudio to identify the tunes she played.

Paris and Chloe put purple candles in the eye sockets of the wallaby skull, lit them, and carried the skull slowly across the room so the candles wouldn't blow out. Emma chanted, 'Here comes a candle to light you to bed.'

'And here comes a chopper to chop off your *head*!' said Paris, looking up at Emma sharply, not smiling at all.

❧

I lay in the dark. I always aimed to stay awake long after everyone else had gone to sleep. If I didn't stay wakeful, and watch over the house, I felt that everything would fall apart.

I thought of the dark outside, the night, everything black, without sun to show the colours. I heard cries, shrill or muffled, of creatures hunting or being hunted. The house lay still, while the cruel world went relentlessly about its business.

I heard mice in the kitchen. I fancied I could hear their claws slipping on the polished wood of the floor. A bat came in and fluttered around my bedroom before flying out again. I heard faint snufflings and snortings as people prepared for sleep.

❧

And the bat goes into each of the rooms in the house in turn and circles three times above the heads of the people in their beds, before flying out again, the sound of its wings a whispered incantation.

I close my eyes. I can see my mother, Emma, who is also awake. She feels the presence of Stella and Paris in the house like an extra weight, as if she carries the whole household inside her body. Unable to sleep, she gets out of bed and stands at the window. She sees Claudio, a dark shape covered by a sheet, roll over in his sleep. She slips into bed beside him and lays her cheek against his back.

I have seen my mother run her hands down my father's back as he stood on the verandah after a shower. She laid her cheek against him then, and I can see now how she loved his compact, muscular body.

❧

My sister Lizzie is also awake. In the dark, unaware of the soft noises of restless people moving about the house, Lizzie reaches under the bed for her guitar. The smooth wood of the neck and the cool metal frets reassure her. She longs to play the guitar so brilliantly that it makes people dizzy. She longs to play as well as Jimi Hendrix, but she knows the absurdity of that; she is just a girl with long blonde hair who lives outside a little town in Australia.

But she imagines the notes she could pull from that guitar if only she could find it in herself to call them up. Lizzie kisses her guitar all the way along its neck.

Only now can I imagine Stella that night. Stella lies in the guestroom, a space enclosed at the end of the verandah. She breathes in all the smells of the night and smiles as she thinks of Claudio's smile, and the intensity and absurdity of his eyebrows. She sleeps naked, and throws off the sheet, and for a moment her body feels the relief of the cool night air.

From the first, it seemed to me I had known about sex. Where we lived, there were always animals mating and producing offspring, and our mother was matter-of-fact about it. When we were still quite young – when I was about six or seven – she told us about men and women making love.

'It sounds *horrible*!' said Lizzie. 'I'm never going to do that.'

'It's not horrible,' said Emma. 'It's nice.' It was a hot day, one of those summer days when the very air oozed moisture. She smoothed the hair from Lizzie's forehead where it hung in damp strands. 'It's lovely to be that close to someone you love. When you're grown-up you'll see how nice it is.'

In those days Lizzie and I shared a bed and slept tumbled together like puppies. That night it was too hot for even so much as a sheet, and Lizzie pushed me away when I tried to curl up close to her.

'Lizzie,' I whispered in the dark, my thumb in my mouth for comfort. 'Does it have to be with a man?'

'What do you mean?'

'Does it have to be with a man?'

'Does it have to be with *anybody*, that's what *I'd* like to know!' she said crossly, and turned her back to me.

I can remember waking the next morning and a close-up of Lizzie filling my entire vision: her cheek, with damp hair lying across it, her nose in profile, one fist held against her face in sleep.

When I thought Chloe and Paris would be asleep, I crept into their room. Because Paris was there I hadn't gone in to talk to Chloe before she went to sleep, as I always did, and I missed her. I knelt beside my sister and listened to her breathing. I shut my eyes and leaned in close to her, taking in her warm, bed-fuddled little-sister smell. Her fat hand lay palm upwards on the sheet and I bent my head to kiss it.

I adored my little sister: if she wasn't one of *us*, part of Lizzie–Laura, she was something far more exotic and lovable.

I became aware that Paris was awake. I stayed for a long time, to spite her, and she didn't breathe, or move, at all.

ॐ

The next morning their room was deserted; they were already out exploring together. On Paris's bed was an exercise book that she hadn't bothered to shut. By sitting on the edge of the bed I could read what she'd written without even touching it.

Yesterday we came to stay with people called the Zucchinis. Laura Zucchini doesn't like me and Lizzie Zucchini doesn't even know I exist. Chloe Zucchini is just a baby but I will be able to make her do what I want.

Mr Zucchini makes eyes at Mum. He looks at her as if he wants to eat her up. He thinks the whole world loves him and that he is the best. Mrs Zucchini is nice and she watches Mr Zucchini all the time as if she thinks he's wonderful too. I hate their toilet, it is a hole in the ground and I always think I'll fall in. There are bats and mice everywhere and their house is like a haunted castle.

Outside, a feral cat had killed a feather-tail glider and eaten it all but for the tail and tiny skull. I found the remains as I made my way down the overgrown track, dense with weeds, that led to my mother's painting studio. It was an old timber shed that leaned into the lantana.

16

I stood at the window and saw Stella reclining on an old sofa, naked, while Emma sketched her. Emma worked quickly, looking up every few moments to study Stella intently.

'Come in, please!' she called, when she saw me. 'I won't have any peepers.'

I crept inside and craned over her shoulder to see what she had drawn.

'Be patient. I'm nearly finished, and then I'll show you.'

I couldn't help looking at Stella's breasts: they were small and pointed, not at all like my mother's, which were plump and soft. It was my first intimation that women could be so different.

My mother had always told me that everyone sees things in their own way – that is why drawings of the same thing are so different. I waited for my mother to finish so I could get an idea of how she saw Stella.

'Now you can look!' she said.

Her sketch had been done very quickly with soft black crayon. It *looked* like a good drawing, but she had merely gone through the motions. It was simply a picture of a naked woman; it told nothing.

My mother has made portraits of Lizzie plucking at the strings of her guitar and everything is there: her beauty and her anxiety captured on the surface of the paper. Those pictures made me fear for Lizzie sometimes. I wanted to capture her beauty, not to keep it for myself, but to contain it and protect her. Perhaps drawing is a kind of capturing.

And now here was this sketch of Stella, which looked like her, but told nothing of what she might be like. My mother can evade even when she draws.

'I like the way you do legs,' said Stella, standing shamelessly naked in front of the easel. 'I remember you, when I was a kid, drawing legs – my mother's legs; remember?'

Emma shot her a smile. 'I learned how to do legs from the illustrations in a storybook when I was a child. I can't remember who the artist was, but she – I'm sure it was a she! – drew the legs with just a couple of swift lines. I liked the curve of the calf, the way it suggested firmness and muscle. Legs are my favourite things to draw. They're so interesting! Because you can never tell from the rest of a person what the legs will be like – have you noticed? Some very slim people have quite big legs. And fat women, especially, can have surprisingly dainty ankles. The legs I hate are ones that are somehow shapeless, with seemingly no muscle in them at all.'

'Fancy hating someone because of their legs.' Claudio stood leaning against the doorjamb. I was embarrassed. It didn't seem right that my father should be able to inspect Stella's nakedness so closely.

Emma glanced at him dismissively. 'I didn't say I hated the people,' she said lightly, 'just the legs.' She began to pack up her materials. Stella pulled on her clothes, lingeringly.

Emma and Stella left the drawing hut, left Claudio standing in the doorway with an expression on his face that was between a grin and a leer. I could see that my father liked women; I thought that perhaps it was the essential thing about him. More than that, he needed women to like and admire him. But I could see that although women liked him, it was not all the time, or when he was in certain moods.

I followed my mother along the path through the lantana. I felt the scratch of the stems against my arm, and smelt the sharp odour of the bruised leaves.

That night my mother and Stella talked for hours in the kitchen. I heard them mention Stella's mother Flora, whom Emma had known for years. She lived just outside Paris still, said Stella.

I'd lived my whole life – an eternity it seemed – in the one place, and it seemed astonishing that someone could have so much mobility. To live near Paris!

The murmur of their voices continued long after I was in bed. They talked with long silences and whisperings and bursts of unseemly laughter, but there was something that told me they weren't really friends.

M

W HEN WE were young we always begged our mother to tell us stories. Real stories, we wanted, of her life.

She only ever told us one. It was a story we loved, and she told it again and again, with variations. Details that were forgotten at one time were remembered at a later telling, so that eventually I built up a patchwork of images and associations which I put together in my imagination into some sort of whole.

It was the story of a magical visit she made when she was sixteen to visit her Great-Aunt Emmeline. That visit was a turning point in her life. It was when she learned to love heat and humidity and tangled, fecund vegetation. The light she portrayed in that story was special: the world was brighter and more marvellous and more . . . *everything*, the way it is sometimes when you look at the colours in the sky at dusk and think *I am in another world*. The story my mother told was about another world.

Her great-aunt lived in a huge old house in the country, eight hundred kilometres north of my mother's childhood home in the suburbs of Sydney. We grew up only an hour or so from where it stood. But my mother never went back to look at it, and never took us to see it. It might not bear being scrutinised, she said, more than twenty years later *in the light of day*. She meant that she wanted to think of it in that special light, the light of memory.

Great-Aunt Emmeline – Aunt Em – was Emma's father's aunt; she had brought him up after his mother died. He died when my mother, Emma, was two and her sister Beth was four; Emma remembered nothing of him.

Their mother didn't visit Aunt Em after her husband's death, and nor did Aunt Em come to visit them, though they wrote occasional letters and there were presents at Christmas and on birthdays. The years just slipped by. Then when Beth was sixteen her mother felt she was old enough to go alone on the train for a visit, and two years later, when *she* was sixteen, it was Emma's turn.

The thing that terrified Emma about going to visit Aunt Em was the idea that once she got there she'd be trapped somehow, and never be able to leave. But a thrill of anticipation went through her as well: that and the terror seemed to belong deliciously together. Until now, she felt, she'd been half asleep, waiting for her life to begin. Here, perhaps, was the great thing she'd been longing for, though what the great thing might consist of she could scarcely imagine.

Beth had set herself up as the expert on Aunt Em, who preferred to be called just Em. Emma always thought of the name as a single letter: M. Beth told Emma that their great-aunt always had a drink of Hospital brandy, standing at the kitchen table, before she went to bed at night. 'Don't let her give you any!' Beth warned.

She said that Aunt Em had been a twin, but that her twin sister had died of scarlet fever when she was still a baby. The nursery door was locked afterwards, and everything kept exactly as it was when the child died. The nursery was upstairs, on the upper floor of the house. Aunt Em lived in the downstairs part only, now, and never went up there.

She said that Aunt Em had a white whisker on her chin, and that it prickled when she kissed you.

And finally she told Emma, in that dramatic voice that bore the unmistakable authority of the older sister, that when Aunt Em died, Emma would have to go and live forever in the vast old house in the country: 'So that there will always be an Aunt Em living there.'

It was a long, rocking, rolling journey north. The train slid through the suburbs of Sydney, gliding surreptitiously along the tracks. It was night, and Emma saw her face reflected in the glass, wan and anxious-looking. She pressed her lips together and looked away. She could smell the cracked varnish of the window frame as she leaned her head against it. The green leather seats were impregnated with the smell of soot. People entering the compartment wrestled with the handle of a door that slid about with the movement of the train. Finally, the lights went off and, surrounded by the smells of strangers, Emma snuggled down under the blanket her mother had pressed upon her for the trip, and slept.

In the morning there were cow paddocks, and kangaroos fleeing through stands of eucalypts. Then the vegetation became denser. The train followed a creek fringed by trees struggling under the weight of vines. The line was cut into the hillsides, and they seemed to be pushing against the forest at each turn. Emma thought she would be swallowed by all that lush, green dampness.

And then she was at Aunt Em's station, a tiny faded weatherboard building surrounded by tree ferns and palms, a station so small it was hardly a station at all, to Emma's city-bred eyes. An old woman waited on the platform, watching alertly. She and Emma recognised each other at once, and would have even if they hadn't been the only people there.

Aunt Em was tall and upright, with a beaky nose and a face that was full of anticipation. She was narrow, with no

hips or breasts, so that her cotton dress was like a pillowcase
for her body, with a belt around the middle. Aunt Em put her
arms around Emma briefly and Emma felt how thin she was,
but strong. The whisker Beth had told her about pricked
Emma on the cheek but she hardly felt it, so overwhelmed
was she by her surprising and sudden arrival after the long
hours of rattling along a track. 'It's so lovely to see you, dear,'
said Aunt Em. She blinked quickly, before turning away.

She had been brought to the station by a neighbour, a
young woman named Flora, who had the longest hair Emma
had ever seen, and the shortest miniskirt, and the nicest legs.
Emma, who loved sketching, felt that she could draw Flora's
legs then and there. But then she was bustled out to Flora's
little Austin, where she met Flora's eight-year-old daughter
Stella, who sucked her thumb and looked with frank curiosity when Emma crawled into the back seat beside her.

Emma took in everything, staring intently from the
window of the car: the winding road with camphor laurel
trees pressing in from both sides, the paddocks full of scotch
thistles and lantana and cattle, the outcrops of bananas on
the hills. There was a sense of things growing headlong in
the heat and the wet. And she was watching for the house,
to see if it was as Beth had said.

It was. She recognised it from Beth's description even
before they turned in the drive. It was set back in a paddock
with hills behind it and a creek winding down one side:
large, two-storeyed, with rusty iron lace on the upstairs
verandah and peeling paint on the timber walls.

From the front door you could see right through the house, down the long shadowy hallway to the back, where there was a concrete path and a rusty water tank illuminated by sunlight. Halfway up the hall was a staircase leading to the upper floor. It was all as Beth had described.

Emma closed her eyes. She wanted the experience of being here to be hers, not a second-hand version of Beth's. The trouble with being the younger sister was that you were never the first to do anything.

Emma opened her eyes and saw Aunt Em looking at her, as quizzical as a finch. 'Are you all right, dear?'

'Oh, Aunt Em . . .' she said. The newness of it all was almost too much for her.

'Just call me Em,' said her aunt, kindly.

Flora came inside with Emma's bag. 'There you go!' she said, setting it down in the hallway.

'Thank you so much, my dear.' Em managed to look both grateful and taken aback. Emma was to grow used to her look of perpetual surprise; all those years of being alive hadn't lessened one scrap her astonishment at the world.

'My pleasure,' said Flora. She put her hands out in a broad gesture of uselessness and shrugged. 'Well, I'll leave you to it.' She clattered out through the front door, trailed after by Stella, who'd only just finished trailing inside, and who gave Emma a lively backward glance as she departed.

≈

The house smelt of lamb fat, and wood smoke, and lavender perfume. The bedroom Emma was to stay in was sparse and clean. It had double doors leading onto a verandah with ancient, splintered boards. There were fresh flowers on a chest of drawers, and a new bedspread. Aunt Em had taken trouble with it. But it was strange, and empty.

Emma had brought her drawing things with her, and Patrick White's *Voss*, which she had imagined reading on long lonely nights in the old house in the country. She'd thrown in a copy of *Das Kapital* for good measure. Emma was an ambitious reader. She unpacked them, along with her small black transistor radio with its earplug. She hoped the radio would have reception. She thought of Aunt Em's place as the end of the earth.

Her meagre things made no dent in the strangeness. Her clothes were swallowed by capacious drawers that had been lined with fresh newspaper, and her copies of *Voss* and *Das Kapital* merely looked as if someone had abandoned them on the night table. Emma went to the verandah door and laid her cheek against the timber doorjamb, listening for the tick of a heartbeat. She felt that such an old house must have a pulse. She rummaged in her bag and found an apple left over from the trip, and she lay on the bed and devoured it, a last link with home.

Out in the hallway, she followed the sunlight till she was outside, and was startled by two pigeons taking off from on top of the water tank next to the door. The sound of their wings was like the squeak of someone running across dry sand. *Yin-yin, yin-yin,* sang the cicadas; their song throbbed inside her head. Emma sighed with satisfaction. Beth had said nothing about all this. The place was hers now.

Em was in the kitchen making tea. It was a gloriously dim, damp-feeling room at the back of the house. Emma peered from the narrow window. There were clumps of lilies growing outside in dark, damp soil. It was so shaded beside the house that no grass grew there. A thrill of attraction and fear had begun in Emma's heart for this place. It was both strange and familiar; it had been waiting for her all along.

Emma pictured herself within this kitchen, within this house, within this damp, luxuriant landscape, and recounted to herself the journey which had taken her further and further from her old life. This was a house of shadows, of dark and light: dark inside, with squares of light where the doors and windows were. The floor of the kitchen and hallway were dark and light too, a chequerboard of tiles. It was a place that she felt she had dreamed about and forgotten.

At a table with a lino top she sat and drank Em's strong, sour tea. Em said, 'Well, my dear. How is your mother? And Beth?' She blinked as she said it, surprising herself again.

'They're well,' said Emma, stirring more sugar into her tea. 'They send their love.' This was true, but sounded as if she'd just made it up, from politeness. Her mother had sent presents, too: a flannelette nightie and a set of face washers, but Emma was shy of presenting them to Aunt Em and had left them in her bag.

'I'm so pleased you could come,' said Em. She smiled and

squinted; she seemed to have trouble with her eyes, for they watered at the slightest thing. 'It's lovely to see Sam's children again. You were such a tiny thing when he brought you here.'

Emma had long had a memory of arriving in a big house in the dead of night. It must have been her father's arms then, that had cradled her in the walk down a long hallway, and up the stairs to bed.

Em peeled a freckled pear and cut it into slices, offering a piece to Emma. It was cold and delicious; the juice ran down Emma's arm and she wiped it away. Em ate the pear elegantly, slicing pieces from it until all that was left was a moist, square core. 'I hope you'll find enough to do,' said Em. 'There's Flora, of course, who lives practically next door. She'll be company for you.' Her voice was high and strange, an old lady's voice.

'I'm sure I'll find enough to do,' Emma told her, smiling down at the table. She heard her own voice, smug and fat with youth. 'I've brought some books, and my drawing things. Anyway, I enjoy a bit of solitude.' She pursed her lips and heard how dreadfully, falsely, grown-up she sounded.

'Your mother said you were interested in drawing. What do you like to draw?' Without waiting for an answer she added, 'You look awfully thin, dear, I think I'll make some toast.' Em got up and stoked the embers of the wood fire into life and cut two thick slices of bread from a white loaf.

'Oh, I draw anything,' Emma told her. 'People, mostly. I'd like to draw you,' she said recklessly, and Em laughed, delighted. '*I'm* no oil painting,' she said.

The toast was deliciously charred. Emma ate it and smiled at Em, who smiled back. Emma observed frankly her aunt's fine, long face and blue eyes. Her white hair was piled untidily on top of her head. They sat there eating toast and smiling and emanating goodwill for some time.

&

In the afternoon Em went to have what she called 'a bit of a lie-down'. She didn't close the bedroom door and Emma, prowling past on her way through the house, glimpsed her lying neatly and sparely on her bed like a package.

Emma had the house to herself.

She went to the kitchen, opened the refrigerator to see if there was anything interesting to eat (there wasn't), and drank a glass of water at the sink, tipping the warmish liquid down her throat with her hand on the tap, her head tilted back and eyes closed. Out in the hallway again she paused, saw a door that was slightly ajar, pushed it right open and stepped inside.

The room was shadowy. It was like being underneath the sea. Heavy red velvet curtains shut out the afternoon sunlight. Only a slit shone between them, but it was intense light from a world that promised solidity. Emma moved the curtains apart a little to let that world in.

Two stiff old armchairs with a design of brown leaves flattened their shoulders to the wall. Between them was a long dark sideboard, gloomy and malevolent-looking. A patterned carpet, so thin it appeared to have grown embedded into the floorboards, filled the centre of the room. The only pretty thing was a glass-fronted cabinet full of china.

Emma closed her eyes and took a breath. She moved without thinking to the curtains and buried her face in them to see if they smelled of redness; she expected them to be luscious, like a ripe plum, but all she got for her trouble was a nose full of dust and mould.

She slid open a drawer of the sideboard and saw a tumble of old letters and photographs. She didn't leaf through them, though she was tempted to. She quickly eased the drawer shut again and it made a sound that caused her to hold her breath.

On top of the sideboard was a collection of framed photographs, their glass frosted with dust. Emma saw a photograph they had a copy of at home, of her father when he was small, standing sturdily under a tree in short pants and a jacket. His long socks were in the process of working their way down his legs. Emma had often gazed secretly at this picture of him, taking it out from the collection of photos her mother kept in a biscuit tin. She longed to know more about him, but her mother had hardly ever spoken of him to Beth and Emma.

He'd been a botanist, lost when he went out alone (as he often did) on a plant-hunting expedition in the Blue Mountains. He was never found; it was as if he simply stepped into the wilderness and it swallowed him up without a trace. Emma's mother kept a photograph of him in his bushwalking gear – khaki shorts and shirt and sturdy walking boots – on the mantelpiece.

Dressed like that he had walked out of their lives.

Emma tore herself away from the photograph of her father and picked up another one. It was a picture of a little girl of about eight with a woman who must be her mother. Emma rubbed her hand across the glass. The dust that coated its surface smeared, so she put her tongue to the glass and licked it. It was cool and thick-tasting. Emma wiped the dust from her tongue and licked again.

They wore clothes from another century, but the child looked as real and as childlike as any child today. Emma knew at once that it was Em. She had a beautiful long face and dreamy eyes. She leaned her head against her mother's breast, and their relation to each other was so tender and private and loving that Emma replaced the picture and tiptoed from the room.

Life with Em in that great old house turned out to be quite unlike Emma's life with her mother and Beth. Home was a very cosy, ordinary, suburban, female nest. Emma's days were filled with the tedium of school and the predictability of watching television at night while her mother knitted, tired after her day in the office. Without a man to feed they often didn't bother with a proper meal, ate macaroni cheese from trays on their laps in front of the television, and afterwards Emma and Beth argued about whose turn it was to wash up. It was secure and safe and dull. Even though she hadn't yet even been able to articulate the desire to herself, it was

34

a life Emma longed to escape from. Here at Em's she was beginning to see she could be someone else. There was time to dream and wander about alone.

One day she woke early, and went barefoot down the chequered hallway in the wake of Em's cat, a slender half-grown kitten with cloudy dark fur. She watched as it wound its questing way out to the dew-damp grass. The house stood, proud and ramshackle in its small square of fenced garden. Cows grazed outside the fence; inside was a garden full of unidentifiable trees, of roses and lettuces, red geraniums and tomatoes, all grown tumbled together in innocent profusion.

Emma put Patrick White and Karl Marx back into her suitcase. She took her sketch pad and went to draw the huge clumps of bamboo that grew near the creek. She tried to capture the smell of the silt and rotting vegetation, drawing the strangeness that she felt.

Flora turned up for the first time since Emma's arrival just as Emma had begun to make a sketch of Em, who was sitting upright and calm, looking out at the garden with her cat on her lap.

'I hope we're not disturbing you,' said Flora, 'but Stella's been pestering me to visit ever since you got here.'

Stella looked with interest at what Emma was doing and said, 'I want to draw, too.' Stella was a slender, eager child, long-limbed and swift; she didn't walk, she darted.

Emma tore a page from her pad and gave it to her with a couple of pencils. Flora went to make tea, and afterwards, while she and Em sat there drinking it, Emma glanced furtively at Flora and indulged the desire she'd had on that first day to draw her legs. She used a few brisk strokes, practising the curve of the calf again and again. She intended one day to draw all of Flora, who had a heavy mass of blonde hair like a thick curtain that covered her behind when she stood up, and a dreamy, voluptuous face.

'What are you drawing? Show me!' demanded Stella, craning her neck to see what Emma had done.

'Legs,' said Emma. She smiled to herself.

'Whose?' demanded Stella. 'Whose legs? And, anyway, they aren't *part* of anyone, they're just legs.'

❧

Emma went to visit Flora. Em directed her to the house, which was just across the paddock – spitting distance, Em said. As Emma appeared in the yard, a wave of half-grown chickens rushed towards her in a happy, welcoming throng. Everywhere she looked there were chooks. They nested in an open shed near the house, some were locked in pens, and others wandered about the yard and the verandah. There were chook droppings everywhere, and the damp yard stank in the humid, festering morning after rain. The chooks were Flora's livelihood. She sold some for meat, and she sold the eggs.

Inside the house there were containers of eggs everywhere, and the smell of chicken blood was pervasive. Stella sat at the kitchen table chewing on a raw carrot. She put it down and Emma could see her little teeth marks clearly, as though a rat had gnawed at it. Then Stella picked up a raw cob of corn and chewed at that, too, keeping her eyes on Emma all the while. She put the cob of corn down, stuck her tongue out at Emma, and ran outside.

Emma stood and rolled an egg around in the palms of her hands. She put it to her nose; it had an animal, earthy smell. 'You can scrape the shit off them for me if you like!' said Flora, coming through the kitchen with a basket of washing. She wore work boots and shorts today, her hair pulled off her face in a glossy ponytail. Emma had only ever seen her when she went out, dressed neatly in a miniskirt, her hair flowing down her back.

Flora's place had the feeling that life was being lived there in exactly the way that she chose. Emma was shocked that she left packets of tampons lying around on the mantelpiece for any casual visitor to see. Later, she simply didn't see the chook droppings on the chairs on the verandah, or the squalor of the house. She saw, though, that an appearance of order could be made out of chaos with the judicious use of an iron before you went out, or a damp washer on a child's face.

Emma loved Flora's clothes. As well as miniskirts and suede boots that came right up to her knees, she had a collection of old clothes that she slipped on from time to time to amuse herself, like a child dressing up. Emma particularly loved an old rose-red shawl with black hibiscus flowers embroidered on it, which Flora flung over her shoulders at the slightest hint of chill in the evening air, giving herself a sultry backwards glance in the mirror. She had a lush black velvet coat that came almost to the floor, and it was so dense and lustrous it was like the pelt of an animal. Flora mourned the fact that the climate was too hot to wear this coat often, but she pulled it on occasionally, and in this coat she appeared to Emma as momentarily dangerous. Flora's clothes were like other skins. In them, she became another person.

One morning, late, Emma arrived to find Flora still in bed, and a young man, bare-chested, wandering around the kitchen making coffee. He brought a cup into the bedroom for Flora. 'Would you like some coffee?' he asked Emma, inclining his head towards her as he bent over the bed.

'No thank you,' she said promptly, though she was almost speechless at his proximity. She was perched on the end of the bed, where Flora had motioned for her to sit. Flora had pulled the sheet up to her neck but Emma could see she was naked underneath. Flora smiled at Emma's confusion and sipped her coffee.

'Emma, this is Frank. Frank, Emma.'

Frank nodded at her and smiled. He had dark skin, and eyes that flashed when he looked at you, and glossy black hair to his shoulders. His chest was firm and muscled, glistening as if burnished. He could have been Greek, or Italian, Emma thought, though he had no accent. She had no experience of people from other places.

'Anyway,' he said, after a few sips of coffee, 'I'd better get going.' He squeezed Flora on the thigh through the bedclothes and left the room. Emma could hear him laughing with Stella as he made his way out of the house;

his laughter was long and loud and without restraint, punctuated by Stella's high-pitched giggles.

When the house was quiet again, it seemed to echo with his absence. Flora reached down and plucked a red silk kimono from the floor. Emma tactfully averted her head while she put it on, though she knew Flora wouldn't have minded if she hadn't.

She had brought her drawing things, and she sketched Flora lounging on her bed smoking a cigarette. She took a lot of care with the detail of the embroidered flowers on the front of the kimono, but was too shy to include the curve of Flora's breast which was just visible at the opening in the front, a curve that she knew she'd find even more challenging than that of her legs.

Emma's deep natural reserve struggled against curiosity and the thrill of an encounter with a handsome young man without his shirt in a woman's bedroom. She said, as casually as she could, 'Are you in love with him?'

Flora hugged her knees to her chest and laughed. 'Love?' she said, and kept laughing as if it was the funniest thing she'd ever heard. 'No,' she said. 'I'm not *in love*, though I love some things about him.'

Emma was ashamed of the way her voice had cracked when she'd asked. She kept her eyes on her page, glancing up at Flora from time to time as she worked. The room was silent, but for the sound of Emma's crayon moving swiftly across the paper.

Though she hadn't admitted it to herself, Emma was

intoxicated by Frank, by his gleaming muscled back and narrow hips, his smile, and especially his laugh; the way he looked at women as if he could consider eating them up. The indefinable but unmistakable smell of sex.

Queen of Swords

So THERE were Stella and Paris, intruding on our summer holidays, filling up the house and taking our mother's attention and wandering endlessly in the garden. I was amazed how two people could fill so much space and be everywhere at once.

Late in the afternoon, with the light seeping through the trees and into the darkened living room, Paris caught me looking at her. She turned her head slowly on her slender neck and then looked away again.

I escaped to Lizzie's room. 'When are they going to go *home*?' I asked her, even though they'd only just arrived.

Lizzie shrugged. She took very little notice of the visitors, and avoided them by going off to the shed where she could

practise the guitar in peace, putting the amp up until there
was a satisfying amount of feedback.

᷾

Paris found plenty to interest her on that long summer
holiday she spent with us. She took Chloe into the hills
where they wandered on narrow paths made by cattle. They
found a dead steer, black with flies. Chloe told me about
it. 'Paris poked it with a stick – poked it in the *bum* where
all the maggots were.'

They found a rotten wallaby carcass that had been
gnawed by wild dogs. Paris managed to detach the head,
and took it back to the kitchen where, unobserved by anyone
but Chloe (hands over her mouth to suppress the giggles),
she boiled it up to clean the meat from the bone. The stench
brought everyone to the kitchen, exclaiming loudly. Paris
told Emma she wanted to have a clean wallaby skull to take
home with her, but Emma took the pot a long way from
the house and tipped it out. 'I think we'll let the ants do
the rest,' she told Paris.

Paris, with her cool, appraising eyes, noted a pleasing
side effect of what she'd done: Emma was annoyed with her.

Later, when she and Chloe were helping Lizzie with the
dishes, Paris deliberately dropped a dinner plate on the floor
while Lizzie was bent over the sink. Lizzie turned immediately at the crash, her plait swinging behind her. 'Stand back!'
she ordered, her arms held out to the sides to ward people
away. Everything Lizzie did was done with solemn intent,

and every shard of crockery and sliver of glaze was swept dutifully into the dustpan.

With Lizzie back at the sink again, Paris took another plate and held it in the air. She motioned to Chloe to do the same, and the plates crashed to the floor at the same time.

'Sorry,' said Paris. 'It was an accident.'

Lizzie began scornfully to sweep up the pieces of broken plate. 'It has to be done properly,' she said, when Paris insincerely offered to help. 'I don't care,' said Paris under her breath, but Chloe felt Lizzie's silent wrath acutely.

'We'd better behave ourselves,' whispered Chloe.

'Not *me*!' said Paris.

Chloe giggled, and they ran to their room, where Chloe collapsed onto the bed hugging herself with delight. She'd found that it was much more interesting to be bad than to be good.

One day Claudio and Stella talked in the dining room for hours after lunch was over. Claudio had stayed behind to sort out some papers. My mother had disappeared to her studio and I thought Stella had gone into the garden for a cigarette. But she had come back and sat down next to him, not right beside him, but with a dining chair between them like a barricade.

Claudio leaned forward across the chair. He talked, holding Stella to him with his eyes. I didn't even try to make out what he was saying. But I watched him.

He bunched his fingers together as he made a point, then opened them again and waved his hand around in a loose arc; he said something that made her laugh; he laughed too, and closed his eyes with a look of bliss. They simultaneously grasped the back of the chair, their hands only centimetres apart.

I walked past and saw my father cast his eyes to the ceiling, a look of intoxication on his face, before he launched into another story.

I crept to Lizzie's room, hoping for an ally, and solace.

'I don't like the way she looks at Claudio.' I whispered it, not because anyone could overhear, but because it was something I'd not even thought properly before, let alone said out loud.

'Who?'

'Stella.'

'They're *flirting* with each other,' she said, her mouth turned downwards with disgust.

Flirting.

I knew instinctively the meaning of this new word.

'Mum hates it.' Lizzie's face was impassive. She had taken to calling our mother 'Mum' instead of 'Emma'. Lizzie picked up her guitar and started to strum it, listening to its resonances with one ear inclined towards it.

I prowled through the dining area one more time. Claudio and Stella were sitting upright now, their elbows on the table. The dining chair stood between them.

❧

It pleases Paris to see the snake. It is thin, black with a red belly, and pours itself down a crevice in a rock wall when she surprises it sunning itself on a path.

Paris watches it disappear. 'Like quicksilver', she whispers. Paris has never seen quicksilver, and isn't even sure what it is, but she is a reading child and the phrase comes immediately to her mind. Seconds later the snake reappears, making its way lightly across the top of the ferns that sprout from the gaps in the rocks. Its tongue flicks in and out. Paris and the snake watch each other with bright eyes.

Chloe and Paris painted each other's faces with tiger stripes. They took off their clothes and painted stripes on their bodies as well. Chloe put a fluffy length of fabric from the dress-up box round her waist, and Paris found an old pink tutu that used to be Lizzie's. It was far too small. The pants climbed up over her bottom and the top didn't cover her nipples.

Chloe led Paris through the undergrowth to a special place she knew, a bowerbird's nest with a treasure trove of blue objects. There was the usual assortment of bits of blue plastic, blue pegs, a faded blue flower. They also found two blue playing cards lying on the ground, face down.

Each had a picture of a queen on a throne. One of the queens was fair-haired and carried a cup like a wine goblet. The other queen was dark, and had a sword. They carried the cards back to where Emma and Stella sat on the verandah.

'Savages!' cried Emma when she saw them emerging from the bushes. She hugged savage Chloe to her, putting her face in Chloe's hair. 'They're tarot cards,' she said. 'I bet they belong to Amrita, down the road. I'll ask her if she's lost them. It'd be typical of her to leave them lying about where a bowerbird could take them.'

Paris looked annoyed.

'But you can keep them for a while,' said Emma. 'They're little treasures, aren't they?'

'What are tarot cards?' said Paris.

'Well, I don't know all that much, but I know it's a special pack of cards that have different things on them to help you think about your life. For instance, *this* card,' said Emma, holding out the fair queen, 'is the Queen of Cups. It could represent a dearly loved female friend. She's good, fair, and creative. She stands for harmony in your life. But if you got *this* card,' Emma held up the dark queen, 'the Queen of Swords, it could mean there's conflict or change or trouble coming to you.

'She's a very powerful queen,' she went on, glancing at Stella with a look that I stored away, so I could work out its meaning later. 'She can bring whirlwinds, tornadoes and gales; she's ardent, deceitful and selfish, never a friend of her own sex.'

There was something about my mother that suggested danger. Stella laughed uncomfortably. 'Quite a lady,' she said.

'I like this one best,' declared Paris, taking the Queen of

Swords. 'Chloe can have the other one.'

Chloe and Paris tossed the tarot cards on the ground, joined hands, and danced in a circle. Then they let go and danced separately, and it became wilder and wilder. Without warning, Chloe ran up to Emma, grabbed her by the hand, and bit her, hard, on the arm.

Emma pulled away with a cry. 'Oh! Chloe! Why did you do that?'

'Because I'm wicked,' said Chloe, and grinned at her, showing her teeth.

'No, you're not, no, you're not,' murmured Emma, and Chloe crept onto her lap, thumb in mouth. Her other hand slid inside Emma's shirt and found a nipple, and she kneaded it between her fingers. My mother cradled Chloe in her arms and rubbed the plump curve of her bare bottom.

Stella pulled Paris onto the sofa, nestling her in the crook of her arm. Paris's pointed little face was stern, her lips pursed. The stuff she'd painted on her body had smudged and worn away, so that she looked merely grubby and uncared for. Stella dreamily kissed her on the forehead.

Late on an overcast day, with storm clouds building, we went to the beach. It was a long, empty beach. The sea was grey and green. I watched my parents walking along the edge of the water. Claudio had taken himself off alone, and his face had a storm-cloud look to it, which I knew didn't mean that he was especially angry or upset; it was just moodiness. His eyes could just as suddenly spark with fire and good humour, and his astonishing eyebrows, one with a zigzag break at the apex, would shoot up towards his receding hairline.

My mother trailed after him, but she eventually caught him up and took his arm, looking in vain into his face as he stared out over the water.

I turned away from them. Stella had also walked up the beach, but in the opposite direction. She walked jauntily, without a care.

I called to Paris, my voice silky. 'How about we bury you in the sand up to your neck? Have you ever done that? It'll be fun – it's so cool in the damp sand.'

I was astonished that she agreed to it. All of us – me, Chloe, Paris and even Lizzie – dug the hole to bury her in, a long hole like a shallow grave so that Paris could lie down flat on her back with her head sticking out. When it was large enough, Paris lay down in it, and we began to fill in the sand around her. I slapped wet sand into the hole with satisfaction; it flew up into her face and made her flinch and blink fastidiously. She looked like an annoyed little cat.

Back at home, the sky dark with storm clouds, Emma threw open all the windows and doors to let the heat out of the house, and wind whipped the curtains and blew newspapers across the living room. As the first lightning shot from the sky, she stood on the verandah with her hair flying and a glass of cold white wine in her hand, and looked at it with satisfaction.

❧

With the storm approaching, Paris lies in the grass with her notebook in front of her, relishing her closeness to the soil, watching ants make their scurrying preparations, diverting them with a stick laid in front of them. With her eyes close to the ground, the world is a thin line, the sky huge. In her notebook she writes three times *I am a witch* and slams it shut.

There is a smell in the air that signals the approach of the storm, and she watches till it is on top of her, till the first lightning darts earthward and rain as pungent as a firecracker falls across her face. Then she stands up and stretches her arms out wide, her face tilted to the sky. She has the power to transform reality.

❧

The storm was wild. Lightning struck the earth next to our house, one bolt so close that a blue streak seemed to appear right inside the living room. The house shook and rocked like a boat in stormy seas. It was exhilarating and frightening; we moved about, peering from windows at the torrents of water. Chloe and I shrieked at each new thunderclap and hugged each other. But we knew that even wild storms finally passed over, so mostly we simply relished the thrill of it all.

The rain washed across the verandah and then eased to a thin drizzle. Then, when it seemed to be all over, the power went off. Paris and Chloe lit their wallaby-skull candle-holder and carried it through the darkened house, their necks bent worshipfully, watching the flicker of the candle. Claudio cooked by the light of a hurricane lantern. He sloshed olive oil into the pan and sang, *'Just take another little piece of my heart now, babee.'* Stella came and leaned on the bench and watched, and he talked to her, laughing loudly. His laughter sounded through the house in bursts. Emma, leaning out over the railing of the wet verandah, turned her head in the direction of the kitchen with a strained smile.

By the time dinner was ready, the rain had stopped and the verandah boards were dark with water that had blown in. It was like the deck of a ship that had survived the pounding of the seas, and we carried the dining table out there and ate in the damp, cool night air, feeling like survivors. Stella sat beside Claudio, and when he said something that made her laugh she rocked from side to side like a child, knocking against him accidentally or on purpose.

Then the power returned, lighting up the house suddenly and surprisingly, for we'd left all the switches on. Chloe and Paris took their candle-holder outside. Chloe had her hand protectively round the flame, watching it, nurturing it against the wind. They found the place where Emma had tipped the wallaby skull onto the ground. Scraps of flesh still clung to the bones, and Paris poked at it with a stick by the light of the guttering candle.

'Paris!' whispered Chloe. 'We could make a spell!'

Before bed I cleaned my teeth on the verandah with water in a cup. Claudio and Emma were standing together, not talking, leaning over the verandah rail looking out into the darkness. I saw my mother press her hand against my father's shoulder, and when they kissed, her tongue slid inside his mouth.

❧

The next morning I went to Lizzie and found her still asleep on top of the bedclothes, with flowers strewn all around her.

She opened her eyes, saw me, and took in the crumpled blossoms. 'Couldn't sleep,' she murmured. 'Went out in the middle of the night to pick flowers.' She closed her eyes and dozed again.

When she woke properly, I was still there. 'Lizzie,' I said. 'Do you think they're going to get a divorce?'

She stared at the ceiling. 'Why do you ask? Nothing's happened. Has it?'

'No,' I replied.

I remembered my mother saying that the Aubergine children had told their parents to get a divorce. These days it was nothing unusual. I knew lots of kids whose parents were no longer together, who had all sorts of living arrangements so that you didn't even quite know who anyone was really related to.

'They don't argue,' I said. I wanted Lizzie to say something else to reassure me.

'I'm so tired,' she said quietly.

She lay staring into the air for a long time, and I asked, 'What are you thinking?'

'Nothing.'

'Go on. You must be thinking something.'

She finally spoke. 'At night flowers have no colour. They are dark, like the night. And some of them have no scent. Is a colour still a colour if you can't see it? Well – you asked what I was thinking. Stupid stuff like that.

'Don't be silly,' she added kindly. 'Nothing has happened. That's it. End of conversation.'

The next morning was sunny, and the grass and trees and sky had an extra brightness, as they do after rain. Emma sat in the kitchen and watched the dappled light on the floor. Yesterday's collection of shells and sea treasures were ranged on the windowsill. She poured a little more tea into her cup and sighed with pleasure.

'I'm going into Mullum for some stuff,' yelled Claudio. 'Anyone coming? But I'm going now! Chop, chop!'

There were shouted negotiations. 'Oh come on, Lizzie!' bellowed Claudio. 'Do you good to get out. Stuck inside with that guitar all the time. *Un*-natural for a young girl!' and then he sang it, operatically: *'Un-nat-ur-al, my dear!'*

Despite myself I got caught up in the excitement of a sudden expedition to town. I ran around getting ready and calling out, 'Wait till I get my hat!', 'I can't find my purse!' But part of me

54

was already making it into a story I could tell someone, sometime, though I didn't know yet who that would be.

'Hurry up, Paris. We'll go without you!' Stella put her head around the kitchen door, where Emma sat calmly with a cup of tea. 'Can I get you anything in town?'

Emma shook her head.

❧

In the end the only ones who didn't go were Emma and Chloe.

The car bumped its way down the track. Paris, in the back with me and Lizzie, stared from the window. She glanced sideways at me with a sour expression, seeming to know when she was being looked at.

'There's a patch we'll go through soon where it's always raining,' Claudio told Stella, who sat with him in the front. 'You watch, even though the day's sunny, it'll shower when we pass through there.'

'See?' he said and they looked at each other and laughed as drops of water spattered over the windscreen. 'It's a regular vale of tears.'

In Mullumbimby we all went our separate ways. 'Do you want to come with me?' Lizzie asked Paris dutifully, but Paris shook her head and stalked off. I saw her later sitting on a seat in the main street, her legs sprawled in front of her, defiantly eating a family-sized block of chocolate, the silver paper pulled back, munching on the whole block without even breaking it into squares.

I went into the second-hand bookshop, where the dust irritated my nose so much I had to leave almost straight away. I examined the plants outside the nursery, and peered into a shop window at earrings arranged in boxes with green felt lining. It was my mother's birthday soon and I had an idea I might buy a present for her. I bought a cupcake at the bakery and walked along nibbling at the icing. I slowed down near the open air arcade and went into a shop full of fake-looking Red Indian stuff: suede fringed vests and dream-catchers made of feathers. There were some tiny cacti with bright flowers that I thought Emma might like. I peeled back the paper case of my cake and devoured the rest, scrunching the paper up into a tiny damp ball.

I saw Stella and Claudio at a table outside the coffee shop. Claudio was talking quickly, waving his arms and laughing, telling Stella one of his preposterous stories. Stella laughed and laughed at Claudio. She giggled uncontrollably and rubbed her arms, as if she was caressing herself.

I looked away, and examined one of the cacti. It had a bright pink flower like a trumpet.

When the sound of the car has died away Emma feels that she can inhabit her house entirely as she wants to. She pours herself through the rooms, becoming thought, feeling, sensation only. The square of sun coming through the kitchen window becomes dappled and disappears. The shadows lengthen. She goes to the cavernous main room, shadowy and cool, and puts her arms round the tree trunk that reaches up to the beams of the roof. It is clay-cold and white and comforting against her cheek. She remembers the grey and green of the sea the day before, the lightning that struck out in bright sparks against the sky, and thinks calmly about going to her studio and attempting to paint it all. But then she decides to simply let it all be, and keep the colours in her mind.

Chloe's singing comes to her, childish and tuneless, and draws her to where Chloe sits on the floor with her dolls, combing their hair and singing and talking to them. Emma wraps her arms around her youngest daughter and smells the farmyard odour of her unwashed hair, the sweetness of her plump limbs. She feels she could drown there, but she releases Chloe after a second or two and returns to the cavern of her house, feels the cool timber floor underfoot, shiny from the tread of all their feet.

When the others return, it disorients her to be so suddenly confronted with the lap and pulse of people around her.

'Couldn't find that size light bulb I wanted,' roared Claudio. 'Bloody useless electrical shop.' He pushed groceries away into the kitchen cupboards, bouncing the doors open, letting them flap like useless wings.

'I got you a present,' I said. I thrust the cactus with the bright pink flower at my mother, unable to wait for her birthday. I'd get her something else, something better, closer to the time.

'What a gloriously coloured flower.' My mother turned and encountered Stella, whose arms were full of dried flowers, large and dun-coloured and as crisp as brown paper.

'For you,' said Stella abruptly. 'For having us,' and thrust the bunch into Emma's hands. Emma automatically put her nose into the arrangement, but there was no fragrance of flower. It was a brown smell, uninviting.

'I think we'll go tomorrow,' said Stella, putting her hands into the back pockets of her jeans. 'We've imposed on you long enough.'

Emma stood holding the gifts she'd been given: the prickly flower and the dead ones, and was about to protest, *not imposed, no*, but weariness overtook her. 'Of course,' she murmured, 'of course.'

That evening, their last evening with us, Chloe presented Paris with the gaudy wallaby skull. 'You can take it home,' she said. Paris took it without a word, dismissively, and Chloe looked so crushed by her ingratitude that I swooped on her and kissed her.

I watched Paris on that last night, taking in everything, imprinting it on her mind. I saw her take note of the uneasiness at the dinner table, where conversation between Stella and Emma was awkward and even Claudio's attempt to crank up laughter fell flat. She saw me looking at her. 'Stare, stare,' she said quietly and carelessly. Another child would have stuck out her tongue, but Paris knew already the power of understatement.

I imagined Paris regaling her friends with tales of this *awful* or *strange* or *weird* or *pathetic* family she'd stayed with. She didn't need the wallaby skull to take away as a memento. As surely as primitive people take locks of hair, or finger-nails, and work bad magic with them, Paris was taking some-thing of our family away with her.

❧

And this is what I had seen that day:

I stood looking at the cactus with the pink flower and then glanced again towards the coffee shop.

Claudio finished whatever it was he was saying, and Stella looked into his eyes. She'd stopped giggling and rubbing her arms and was absolutely still. Claudio said something else. He didn't laugh as he said it. Stella lowered her eyes and replied. Her hand reached across the table and took his. She took my father's hand, the hand I knew so well with its square fingers and short, tough nails.

My father closed his eyes. He looked happy. *Thank you,* I saw his lips say. *Thank you.*

With his other hand my father reached out and touched Stella's cheek with the back of his fingers.

I bought the cactus with the pink trumpet flower and went looking for Lizzie. I found her a few doors away in the op shop. She was trying on an assortment of dresses out in the open shop, not bothering to take off the clothes she was wearing first.

I told her I had seen Stella and Claudio having coffee, but I didn't tell her what else I had seen.

'You should have seen her,' I said. 'She was laughing like a hyena.' I could feel my mouth pull into a grimace and my teeth bare like a hyena's itself as I said the word.

❧

After dinner I sat in Lizzie's room with her. 'Anyway,' she said with satisfaction. 'They're going tomorrow.'

She plucked a string of her guitar and listened as the sound resonated and then died away.

'And nothing happened,' she said.

I wondered if the sound of the guitar was still there, though we couldn't hear it. You can only hear music when it's played but it's still an event. It's still real. I imagined the sound wave passing out into the universe. Perhaps someone was still hearing it somewhere.

❧

That evening I found Paris staring at a snake in the grapevine. I stood beside her and watched it. Its eyes were milky, and I thought it might be blind, though it had turned its head to face us.

I experienced its sinewy strength as if it were my own body, and was contained and held tight by the cool green

60

of taut skin. We stayed there together for a long time, the snake coiled surreptitiously in the grapevine and Paris and I eye to eye with it.

When Paris finally reached out to touch it, it slid away.

The next morning, early, just as Paris and Stella were about to leave, both of us thought at the same time to go to the grapevine to look for it. We found a snake skin, silvery and arrowed with scales.

'She's shed her skin!' Paris whispered.

I reached out to touch it. The skin was not dry, but soft, and where it was rucked and folded near the head, still as moist as a living thing.

Trailing Clouds of Glory

'Tell me about the olden days,' my mother asked Aunt Em one day, trying to winkle something out of her, but Em waved her question away with a laugh.

'Oh, I never talk about what happened in the past. I'm only interested in what's happening now,' she said.

They sat in the sunroom off the kitchen, Em in her favourite floral armchair, Emma in a low-slung cane chair painted bright orange, though the paint was cracked and peeling away. She could see why Em lived in only a part of the house; it was simply too big for her. She confined herself to the kitchen and sunroom, her own bedroom and the verandahs, and these were kept as up-to-date and cheerful as she could manage, with a new radio on a shelf in a corner of the kitchen, and current magazines and newspapers piled untidily in a rack in the sunroom.

On the whole Em wasn't a great talker; she was content for Emma to simply keep her company. She liked to see Emma doing whatever she pleased, which was mostly dreaming away the afternoons in the garden with her sketch-book. Emma often caught her intelligent, beaky gaze resting on her with approval. But sometimes Em looked as dreamy and as wistful as the child she'd once been.

Every afternoon Em took a nap to keep her strength up, and Emma got used to having the place to herself. She resisted the urge to see the top floor of the house, to see if there *was* a room kept for all those years unchanged since Em's twin sister had died. But she crept to the living room that Em never used and wiped the dust from all the framed family photographs, staring at the pictures of her father, trying to see something of herself in them. She gazed wonderingly at the picture of Aunt Em with her mother, at the way the light from that long-ago time fell through the slatted blind onto their faces. Emma felt a tenderness for them, and for Em as she was now, that surprised her.

But she often surprised herself now with new sensations and feelings. Her life in the house was all sensation and image, rich and heady. Here, she was so different from the Emma who lived with her mother and Beth that she could forget about who she was, and be simply a bundle of nerve endings.

She grew used to the sound of Em's radio coming from the kitchen in the early mornings, which she blocked out with the tinny sound of her own transistor through the earplugs. There were songs that were played over and over that Emma liked: 'Have you seen your mother, baby, standing in the shadows?' Or was it 'lover'? Emma couldn't tell.

Aunt Em knew things. There were words for everything that surrounded her ancient crumbling house. Birds that came to the garden were spangled drongoes or rainbow bee-eaters or fire-tail finches or striated pardalotes. Trees were tamarinds or quandongs or red kamalas. When Emma murmured that they all sounded exotic, Aunt Em's eyes grew bright with amusement. 'They're not at all exotic,' she said. 'They belong here. It's the roses that are exotic.'

The black phone on the wall rang twice while Emma was staying there: her mother and Beth, ringing to see how she was. She stood and listened to their distant voices as she stared up the dim reaches of the staircase.

❧

It was summer, and it rained – sometimes a foggy mist crept down from the hills in the morning, sometimes there was an evening torrent preceded by thunder and lightning. Emma stood on the verandah when it stormed, watching the lightning shoot down to earth, loving it. And there was the humidity, always, that coated your skin with a slick of sweat. She went outside on damp nights, and wandered around the yard, listening to the sound of cicadas and watching for fireflies, whose pulsing trails she followed into the trees. She followed the moon too, watching it move around between the trees; sometimes it caught in the branches, and then broke free and escaped high into the sky. Each night she watched as, little by little, it waxed or waned. On still nights she thought she could hear the sound of the sea, which Em said was just over the hills. It was a gentle swooshing sound like blood moving through veins.

One night late, Emma stood in the garden and watched as Em poured her evening drink of Hospital brandy (the brand with medicinal overtones), standing at the kitchen table. She sipped it slowly and with enjoyment. Emma saw the scene as a picture: the kitchen window was the frame, the darkness was a border that set off the tableau inside the house. In the daytime, the house was dark, and the light outside contrasted starkly, but at night it was the opposite, and that was why she went out there, to drink it all in and marvel at the difference. *Woman In Kitchen, Night, 1960s* would be the title of the picture, had Emma ever painted it.

Her nights were never sweeter. She lay on her bed with the sheet kicked off, wrapped in the soft darkness, veiled by a mosquito net, aware of the relief of night air flowing over her skin, and of Aunt Em asleep in her own bed, lying as straight as a board. The house towered above her, mysterious and hidden, but the small part that she and Em inhabited sang with their small daily pleasures.

≈

One afternoon she came upon Flora and Stella bathing in the creek. She called out to them and sat down on the bank to watch. They had lathered themselves with soap, their hair as well, and were splashing and laughing and tickling each other. Flora suddenly caught Stella up in her arms, and stood there cradling her, waist-deep in water, gazing into her eyes. Then just as suddenly she kissed her on the forehead and released her back into the water; Stella submerged and came up gasping like a fish, water streaming over her face, her hair slicked back. Emma remembered the picture of Em with her mother, taken all those years ago, and she thought, *nothing lasts*. She was full of loss and longing; she wallowed in it, stretching out on the bank and staring up through the branches of a tree, watching the pinpoints of light through the leaves.

Emma loved this place, but it had a tendency to make her melancholy. She'd taken to going for walks in the early evening, and she saw symbols everywhere of the vulnerability of life. The sight of a calf alone on a distant hillside, tottering on unsteady legs with no mother in sight, crows circling overhead, had made her sad for days.

'Come into the water, Emma,' Flora called. 'It's lovely. Take off your clothes and come in.'

But Emma shook her head.

She lay in the grass and dreamed about love, for Emma was a great believer in Love. It was Beth who pinned pictures of the Beatles on her bedroom wall and declared on many mornings that she'd had 'another lovely dream about Paul last night', but it was Emma who yearningly remembered the lyrics of their song 'Love Me Do', despite her averred interest in *Voss* and *Das Kapital*.

The grass was long and full of seeds that fell down her back, and ants wandered along various parts of her body, causing her to itch. She brushed them all away and continued to lie with her nose close to the ground, drinking in the earthy, herbal smell.

She thought of Frank, his glistening back as he dug in Flora's garden, the corded muscles of his arms, his ready, noisy laugh. She had asked Flora, had pressed her, about whether she loved Frank, whether she'd marry him, but Flora waved the idea away. She'd said, lazily, 'Stella and I are all right.'

But Stella loved Frank. She hung onto his arm and pestered him until he noticed her; she giggled helplessly when he tickled her. She sought his attention by dressing up; one day she appeared in her mother's long black velvet coat. It swept the floor and enveloped her like a shroud, but she had her mother's sense of style and she wore a beret on her head and nothing at all underneath, and she looked pleased when Frank wolf-whistled her.

Flora took them all to the beach, just a short drive away, late one afternoon. She said she only ever went late, when the sun was going down, her skin was so fair. 'First to see the sea!' called Stella, as they crested a hill and saw the ocean stretched out in the near distance.

Emma strolled along the shore, and the white moon hung low in the sky. Still in her melancholy mood, she saw death everywhere: a long thin seahorse, as stiff as a twig; a fish with its eyes pecked out by gulls. Everywhere was the smell of rot overlaid with the clean smell of salt. Aunt Em, so old and upright, walked a little way along the shore, and then stood still, and gazed at the sea. She searched the tide line for treasures and looped her skirt up into a nest to hold the things she wanted to keep. Her old legs were as mottled and as pleated as tree bark. Flora wore a white bikini, and her skin was white; she was lush and full and ripe. She caught wave after wave, with the white full moon behind her on the horizon. And then she dragged Stella into the sea from where she'd been dabbling on the edge. Emma saw their two blonde heads bobbing close together far out among the waves.

'Do you think there was someone in her life she was to marry? You know, who got killed in the war or something?' Emma asked later, as Flora lay stretched beside her on a towel. She was sure there had been a young man in Em's life, a great, tragic, lost love.

'Who? You mean Em? I don't know. Maybe. Maybe there wasn't. Do you think there ought to have been someone?'

Emma didn't reply to that. Instead, she said, 'What did Em do, then?'

'Do?' said Flora.

'For a job. When she was young. With her life.'

'I don't know,' said Flora. 'There wasn't much for a lot of women *to* do in those days, was there? Look after other

71

people's children, or do domestic work, or factory work if they were poor. If they were rich, maybe try to write or paint, if they took themselves seriously enough. But her family had money, didn't they? That house . . . and they were lawyers, weren't they? Her father and her brother, at least. There was family money. Maybe she didn't have to do anything.'

'She looked after my father,' said Emma. 'She brought him up when his mother died.'

'There you go, then.'

'But apart from looking after him, what did she do – you know – to fill in her days?'

Flora rolled over onto her stomach and regarded Emma with amusement. 'She lived,' she said.

Emma had almost forgotten that there was an upstairs to go to. The dark staircase reminded her sometimes, but she came to almost regard it as a decoration, something that had no real purpose.

As she wandered from the house one afternoon she discovered something that was like another room, it was so self-contained and private. In the middle of the paddock at the back of the house was a large circular clump of trees like a small forest. Emma pushed her way inside, first broaching a wall of pungent lantana that scratched at her arms and face, reminding her of the bramble hedge that surrounded the castle of the Sleeping Beauty. The lantana gave way to trees with tall trunks that made a canopy overhead excluding the sunlight; under them were vines and ferns and countless small plants. At the centre of this room of trees was the beauty – a great tree with a buttressed trunk and branches reaching out to the sky.

Emma returned later with her sketchbook and drew this tree, which she saw as a great muscled human torso, sinewy and strong. She looked up at it, and sketched, and looked up, and sketched, and put down her book to wrap her arms part way around its trunk and breathe in the smell of it. She thought and didn't think of Frank's naked back, the movement of his muscles as he worked in the garden. Those were dangerous thoughts and she both refused and welcomed them, and she put all her suppressed feelings into her drawings of the tree. They became almost human portraits.

With the rough drawings spread out beside her on the verandah, Emma tried to make a final picture. Her crayon rasped softy and swiftly across the paper. In the garden a spangled drongo glittered. Em sat back in her chair, a hair-brush in her lap.

'I see you've found your father's forest,' she said. There was absolutely no weight in her voice at all, no inflexion to help Emma discern her feelings about what she said.

Emma didn't look up; the crayon flashed a confident line down the curve of the trunk. 'Tell me about it,' she said. Emma knew then that she was right, that the clump of trees she'd found was a kind of room where she could discover things.

'It wasn't always a forest. It was just that fig tree at first,' said Aunt Em, her voice airy and detached, as if this was ancient history. 'The one you're drawing. That was all that was there. It was all that they left when they cleared the land. Sam and I used to walk up there and sit in the shade. But when he was – oh, only about nine or ten – he saw that there were seedlings coming up beneath it.'

Now Aunt Em's face was puckered with the pleasure of remembering, her eyes narrowed. 'And he said to me, "Auntie, these little plants must be from seeds the birds have dropped after they've eaten fruit from the trees in the hills." And he said we should make a fence round the fig so the cattle couldn't eat the seedlings.

'So that's what we got his father to do – Sam wanted the fence put some way out from the fig to allow the trees room to spread. He pestered and *pestered* me to get him books about plants.' Em laughed with pride. 'He was such a clever boy. He learned how to identify them by looking at the leaves and so on. And he went into the hills where the scrub hadn't been cleared and brought back seeds himself, from trees he found there, and he raised them up and planted them along with all the seedlings left by the birds.'

'And all these years later they're all still here,' said Emma.

'Yes,' said Em. 'And he knew they would be. He said to me, "Auntie, when we're all long dead these trees will still be alive. That fig has already lived for a hundred years or more." Oh, he loved trees. And he didn't want to be a lawyer like his father and grandfather. He said he'd die if he sat in an office all day. He liked going out to where it was wild. He dreamed of finding a new species, a plant that no one had discovered. He said there were still plants out there that hadn't yet been identified.'

Emma glanced quickly at Em's face and then back down to the drawing of her father's fig. Em didn't look sad; her face was calm, clear, remembering. Her hairbrush was forgotten on her lap, her hair awry and only partially unpinned.

Emma put her sketchpad aside and stood up. With one hand on her great-aunt's shoulder, she leaned forward and took up the hairbrush from her lap. She removed the last few pins from Em's hair and began gently to brush it out. She noticed the pale skin of her scalp, the delicate whorls of her ears, the fine strands of white hair, and she was breathless with awe that you could be this close to someone.

Ever so slightly, Em leaned against Emma's body. 'He was such a funny little boy,' said Em. 'When I arrived to look after him when his mother died, he said in the kitchen on the first morning, when I was about to cook breakfast, "Don't you use my mother's saucepans!"' She laughed at the memory.

Emma moved in front of Em and knelt down. Aunt Em's skin was so lined and wrinkled that her face seemed decorated with a beautiful deliberate pattern. She put her hand at the side of Em's face, smoothing the hair over her ears, so that all she could see of Em now was her face. Em's eyes looked steadily back at her and Emma held the gaze, wanting to remember, wanting to capture this particular view of Em so that she'd never forget. Then quickly Emma stood up, kissed Em on the forehead, said 'All done!' and put the hair-brush back into her lap.

Em took up the hairpins and put her hair up again. She needed no mirror; it was something she'd practised for most of her eighty-three years.

❧

When Emma, alone in her room that night, drew a portrait of her great-aunt from memory, the whole page was filled with a face, not the whole face, but the part around the eyes. And her drawing wasn't symmetrical, but slanted and partial, and when she'd finished, it wasn't a picture of an old woman at all but of a child.

❧

At the beginning Emma had counted down the days till she could leave, but now she found she didn't want to go home. She loved it here with Em. And miraculously she became ill, just a day before she was to go. She came down with a fever, felt dizzy, sweated, then felt as cold as ice. Perhaps it was all that wandering around on humid nights, coming in with her hair beaded with raindrops, that did it.

She floated on a wave of illness. Aunt Em called the doctor, who said she should rest, and have plenty of liquids. Flora came, and changed the tangled, damp sheets for cool crisp ones. She changed Emma's nightie for her too, when she was too weak to even lift it over her head. Stella brought grapes, carrying them into the room reverentially in a cut-glass bowl.

At last, in the middle of one morning, Emma woke from sleep and felt well, and strong. She got out of bed and found that she could walk. But once she was up she found she wasn't strong, she was weak. She went out onto the verandah. Em was in the garden, a pair of clippers in her hand. Emma watched as she drew a red rose towards her and, with her eyes closed, breathed in the scent. Emma saw how surprised and pleased she was at being alive.

✌

Emma got up at dawn the following morning and put on a long red dress.

In a red dress and in her bare feet my mother, aged sixteen, walked across the paddocks till she was within sight of the sea.

The sun was not quite up. The grass was moist, and it wet her feet and the bottom of her dress. She walked, avoiding cowpats, ducking under barbed wire fences, looking at the marvel of dewdrops on spider webs until, breathless, over an hour later, she came upon the argent ribbon of the sea stretched out on the horizon.

Argent was the word she used to describe it to herself. It was a word with overtones of heraldry and mediaeval heroism, a colour you might find on a shield, or a coat of arms. The sea was a crumpled silver, as if someone had screwed it up and then straightened it out again and laid it in that space where the sea meets the sky. Then, having sighted the sea, she stopped to catch her breath, and turned round and walked back, 'trailing clouds of glory', she told herself (a line she'd got from a poem). It was an easier walk, being mostly downhill, but this time the sun was hotter and higher. She paused to pick bits of grass to chew on, and flowers she liked the look of – weeds, mostly – so that by the time she reached Em's house she was trailing not only glory but various bits of vegetation as well.

The house was silent. Emma went to the kitchen and put on the electric jug for tea. When it was made (and this was the first time she'd made tea for Em, who usually got up first) she took a cup to Em's room. Em was lying in bed, with her hands folded neatly across the white cotton sheet. It was the way she slept on her afternoon naps: neat, spare, contained within her body as though it were a box. But now there was something different about her. Em was dead.

Emma sat the cup down on the bedside table (it shook, and spilled into the saucer) and touched Em gently on the hand. Em's skin was the texture and colour of a dried leaf that Emma had collected on her walk: papery, mottled, delicately veined. When Emma had held the leaf up to the light, the paler patches proved to have almost worn away; the light showed right through them. Emma lifted Em's hand and laid it gently down again. Then she left the room, not knowing what to do.

She went to the foot of the stairs and paused, her hand on the banister. Then decisively (though she didn't decide; she didn't even think), she went up the stairs two at a time till she reached the top.

There was no locked room. There was no nursery left exactly as it had been when Em's twin sister died over eighty years before. There was, in fact, very little furniture and a lot of dust and dirt. The skeleton of a bird lay in a fireplace, a few tattered black feathers still intact.

Emma pushed up a window. It was stiff and difficult to shift and made a noise she wanted at once to stifle, it was so loud in the stillness of the house. Fresh air flowed in, and she stood with the breeze on her face. From her vantage point she could see right over to Flora's house. She saw Flora and Stella come out of the house together, and the chooks come crowding around them. She thought she could hear their voices. In a little while she would go across the paddock and tell Flora that Aunt Em was dead, but for now she would just stand at the window and look out.

Em is dead and she is a child having her photograph taken with her mother on the verandah. The light falls through a slatted blind onto their faces. She is a young woman about to cook breakfast for her nephew who says, 'Don't you use my mother's saucepans.' He is a child planting a forest around the central core of a vast, maternal fig. He is lacing his boots and setting out on a plant-hunting expedition and his body will never be found. His widow sits in resignation and knits in front of the television. His daughter stands at the top of his childhood home and thinks how all time is simultaneous; everything is happening at the same time and forever.

'Whose legs?' demands Stella. 'And anyway, they aren't part of anyone, they're just legs.'

Aunt Em goes inside to make more tea. And Flora seizes Stella by the hand and they waltz along the verandah and inside the house, down the hallway through the shadowy interior to the blinding light at the back door and back again. Emma gets up to watch, seeing the shape their two bodies make together, a whirling circle with hands clasped high; they are two indistinct female figures.

Em is arrested in the act of slicing a long brown pear down the middle by Flora, who takes her laughing and protesting for a slower whirl, leaving the two halves of the pear and half a pawpaw and the steaming teapot on the kitchen table.

A rooster crows from Flora's farmhouse over the way and a black and white dog, a border collie owned by the man who comes to do the garden, runs round and round outside on the grass.

Em's cat has curled up on the seat of a bentwood chair. The pear sits on the table, long and narrow at the top, as curved as a woman below its waist, a pattern of black seeds at its core. The dog is black and white and so are the tiles. The roundness of the twinned dancers is echoed in the pawpaw. Emma is taking all of this in so she can perhaps paint it one day – all the patterns and resonances – when Stella comes to her and, with an expression of slow delight, holds out her arms for Emma to join in the dance: join in and not just be a watcher. And Emma takes Stella in her arms and is at once astonished by the child's thinness and lightness: Stella is insubstantial and fine and strong and Emma is reminded of Aunt Em when she hugged her at the station.

When they finish their dance and come to rest at last in the sunlight on the back step, Flora applauds and exclaims, 'Stella's a star!' And Stella smiles and impulsively reaches up and kisses Emma full on the mouth. Emma pushes Stella away, shocked by how soft and innocent and erotic a kiss can be.

Butterflies

THE YEAR I started high school I went about with a red woollen beanie pulled down over my ears. I wore it night and day, in school and out, despite the heat of summer. The school wasn't strict about uniform, and a lot of girls wore woollen beanies that year.

'You'll overheat your brain,' said Claudio. 'It will make you stupid.' I stuck out my tongue at him and rolled my eyes in towards my nose.

I came home from my first day at high school and stood alone in my room. *This will go on for six years. Six, whole, never-ending years.* Six years seemed like the rest of my life. It wasn't that I minded school. It was simply the thought of the never-endingness of day following day, each of them the same. The inevitability and rhythm of it.

The red beanie was a comfort. I knew it made my face look fatter, but it flattened down my mop of curls. I liked the snugness over my ears, the give of the wool as I hauled it on over my head. It gave off a comforting animal odour, a sheepy but human smell. It wasn't feminine. I could be a woodcutter in that hat, or a fisherman.

❧

'Lucky thirteen,' Lizzie said on my birthday. But I didn't feel lucky. I felt stolid and stodgy. I wanted wonder and excitement and difference. I wanted to be outrageous and outsize and out of bounds. *Magic Happens* said stickers I saw on the backs of cars and kombi vans. *But when*, I wondered, *and how.*

❧

Lizzie saw a notice on a board in Mullumbimby:

FEMALE DESEXED CAT NEEDS HOME
LIKES TO BE ONLY ANIMAL
GOOD RATTER
HER NAME IS ARTEMIS

Without warning, she arrived home with Artemis in a cardboard box.

'Oh Lizzie,' sighed Emma. 'It'll kill birds.'

'She,' said Lizzie. 'She's a she. And she's a good ratter.'

Artemis shot out of the box and around the kitchen like a firecracker, and finally came to rest on top of the refrigerator, which was to become her preferred place, amongst the bottles of rescue remedy and pots of tiger balm.

Claudio was away camping in a forest, filming people chaining themselves to bulldozers. He arrived home late one afternoon with his crew and a van full of wet tents and a week's worth of washing.

He exploded when he saw Artemis. 'A bloody cat!' Claudio often spoke with exclamation marks.

Artemis perched on the refrigerator and glowered at him. She had a head for heights. Claudio glared back at her.

'She's a good ratter!' Lizzie told him.

'Artemis, wasn't she some . . .' – Claudio wrestled with a bottle of red wine and a corkscrew – 'bloody . . . goddess of fecundity or something? We'll end up with thousands of cats!'

'She's desexed.' Lizzie was at her most powerful when she spoke quietly.

Claudio didn't push the point; the house was full of guests. The van had spilled them out, along with the wet tents and the washing, and a pile of film equipment. Damp people milled about with their hands in their pockets, gazing up at the impossible height of the ceiling and shrugging the rain off their jackets. Claudio and his crew were full of camaraderie after their week together in the mud and wet. I noticed a girl with a round face and hair bright with orange henna. There was also a thin, tall boy I liked the look of, with a pale, lightly freckled face and very pale red hair.

Claudio seated his guests around the dining table, pouring wine for everyone. He downed a glass quickly and poured another, then leaned back in his chair.

'The cat's name is Artemis,' he told the girl with orange hair. 'Who, if I remember rightly' (leaning towards her intimately) 'was the goddess of fecundity. There's some ancient statue (circling one hand in the air) – tits all over her chest! But –' (he suddenly remembered) 'bloody hell, wasn't she meant to be the *virgin* huntress? How could she be both?' Claudio sat up and looked around at no one in particular, outraged. He hated ambiguity. He hated a pause in the flow of his words even more. 'Anyway . . . *this* Artemis is desexed, so there won't be much fecundity, but I'm told she's a good ratter – that's where the huntress bit comes in, I suppose!'

He roared with laughter, and the girl with orange hair, whose name was Amanda, smiled uncertainly.

'Actually,' said Lizzie, who stood with Artemis in her arms and regarded Claudio disdainfully, 'Artemis's virginity wasn't about her sexual purity, but a reference to her being complete in herself, inviolate.' Lizzie had been studying up on Artemis; she'd known Claudio would make a thing of it.

All the young men in the crew looked at her with admiration and lust. In the golden light from the lamps, with her hair shimmering over her shoulders, she had the kind of beauty and great height that made her scorn magnificent and imperious. But Lizzie didn't notice them. She picked up Artemis and stalked off to have a shower.

My mother looked at the pile of washing that had been

dumped on the verandah and then out at the rain. The crew stuck close by Claudio in the living room; you could see that, having endured the hardships of a protest camp for a whole week, they felt bonded together for life. Emma left them to it. She went into the kitchen and made food.

'And what do you do?' asked Amanda, as Emma sat finally, exhausted, over a plate of pasta. 'Are you a filmmaker too?'

I watched. My mother hated this question: the assumption that because Claudio made films, she must too, except that she was so hopeless at it that no one had ever heard of her.

'No,' said Emma. 'No, I don't.'

'What do you do?' said Amanda. She ate delicately and fastidiously.

'Oh, this and that,' said Emma, vaguely, sipping her wine and staring out at the rain.

The boy with the pale hair and skin looked shyly at me and smiled. He had been eating his meal with frank and grateful hunger. I thought that although he had looked at Lizzie with admiration as the others had, there had not been so much lust there.

Claudio plunged the corkscrew into another bottle of wine. '*It's now or never,*' he sang, '*Your soul or mine.*'

Lizzie arrived at last from her long shower, and stood in the doorway with Artemis in her arms. Her hair was wet, plastered down unflatteringly over her head.

'Well, she's *my* cat,' she announced, 'and don't any of you dare, ever, to say a word against her!'

⁂

Artemis was a wild and wiry little animal, and took as much of a dislike to Claudio as he had to her. If he came near her when she was eating she growled at him threateningly and hunched over her food.

One night a tiny bent-wing bat found its way into the kitchen and flopped onto the floor. Artemis, opportunistic, caught it.

I heard my mother's cries and ran in. Artemis let go of the bat at once and escaped through the window over the sink, her hind legs flicking away into the night like a shadow spirit's.

I held the bat in the palm of my hand. The fur was the colour and texture of a velvet dress my mother had worn at one time to parties. There was a suggestion of gold amongst the brown. I looked into the bat's face. It was as intricate as an ear, and ancient, and wild. The tiny chest contained a still-beating heart, but it grew fainter, and, as I watched, it became still.

I have seen the last breath of a bat. It was a thought both horrible and wonderful, and it made me slightly breathless myself.

In the morning I helped Chloe bury the bat in the garden. 'Pipi*strello*,' I said lingeringly, saying the Italian word that Claudio had taught me. 'Pipistrello,' echoed Chloe, as she sprinkled earth over the small corpse. Soil fell into its eyes and nostrils, and I turned away, unable to watch.

Lizzie refused to have anything to do with the burial; she said why shouldn't Artemis have killed the bat if it had flopped down into her clutches like that? She said haughtily that the bat must have had a *death wish*, and implied that Artemis was the unwitting and innocent agent. And she cradled Artemis protectively in her arms and strode off to her room.

Chloe and I made a shrine of rocks and flowers for the bat, and that seemed to be that.

I came upon Artemis later, sitting on a fence post with a knowing look on her face. She allowed me to go right up to her and stare intently into her eyes. *Do cats eat bats? I asked her silently. Do bats eat cats?* It seemed that with all the looking into Artemis's eyes, for a moment I became a cat.

That night I woke to the sound of singing, and it was so persistent that I got out of bed and went outside.

It was Lizzie, standing alone in the night (I would like to remember moonlight, but there wasn't much of it that night, if I am to be truthful), and she was singing, something she hadn't done for ages. I felt certain she was making it up as she went along; it was a wonderful song, full of unexpected twists and turns and consisting not of words but merely of sounds. Lizzie stood outside in the dark, *lifting up her voice in song*, which is the way I see it now, though at the time I was only aware of my sister standing tall in the night, singing as the spirit moved her. She didn't notice me watching from the shadows, and I didn't reveal myself, aware that here was the kind of marvellous thing I had been looking for in my life. I didn't want to spoil it.

❧

Unexpectedly, the next marvellous thing came from my own body, the way a spider unwinds the magic of silk.

Our family was swimming in the creek. We never bothered with costumes there, and I sat on a rock above the swimming hole lazily watching everyone splashing in the water. I had a familiar, heavy, almost pleasurable feeling in the bottom of my belly and I sat and luxuriated in it. And then came the warm sticky trickle between my legs. I had been menstruating for over a year now, and I enjoyed the rhythm of it, the small drama of discovering blood on my pants every month. I sat and allowed the blood to seep out onto the rock and onto the top of my thighs, and then I thought I should dive into the water to wash it off.

I stood up. For one instant my thighs were stuck together by congealing blood and I felt the tiny resistance as they pulled apart. Looking down, I saw a red butterfly on my legs made of blood. A symmetrical pair of wings, like an ink blot of folded paper, but coming from inside me: made unexpectedly by my own marvellous body.

'Lizzie!' I called. 'Look! A butterfly!' I pointed to my legs.

Lizzie turned to me, wiping water from her face with both hands, uncovering her eyes like someone playing peek-a-boo. I saw her expression, shocked for just one heartbeat, and then because I was laughing so much she began to laugh as well.

I flapped my legs a few times to show how the butterfly could fly, and then I dived into the water and it vanished.

❧

My life was not all wonderful at this time. There was often tension in the house, between Lizzie and Claudio, and Claudio and Emma. I felt I was stuck in the middle, watching it all.

Artemis killed a snake and left it on the kitchen floor. It was a small red-bellied black snake, and she left it belly uppermost, so that it was like a length of red ribbon that someone had casually dropped on the floor. The belly had a softness that I hadn't associated before with snakes. I could see that it was a creature with insides, that in that long, soft belly were the same vulnerable workings that kept all animals alive.

'Has that cat actually killed a rat yet?' said Claudio that evening. 'It seems she has a talent for killing anything but.'

Lizzie looked at the plate of fish that Emma had put in front of her. Lizzie was a strict vegetarian, but she made an exception for fish.

'You know, I've been having doubts about fish,' she said, and pushed her plate away.

'Ye gods and little fishes!' It was Claudio's attempt at humour, but he was too close to being a parody of himself at his worst, when he could explode with sudden anger. Lizzie got to her feet and went out without a word. Emma looked at Claudio, unsmiling. She always said he didn't want to tell when Lizzie was being serious, when something was of utmost importance to her.

When I'd finished eating I followed Lizzie to her room. I wanted to console her. I wanted to be consoled. Lizzie was hunched over her guitar, her ear close to its body, plucking the strings softly in a disconsolate way. She seemed to be listening to the guitar, waiting for it to tell her something.

❧

Now that I was at high school I had made a friend apart from Lizzie. Her name was Alice. She lived in town, she played a silver flute, and she had glossy black hair that was cut into the nape of her neck and looked like a little cap.

I invited her out to our place for the day and I didn't know quite what to do with her. I showed her how to make little towns in the earth, with log cabins constructed of sticks, and trees made from the tips of casuarina branches the way Lizzie and I used to, but it seemed too childish a game and we abandoned it.

'What do you want to *do*?' I asked in desperation, and she shrugged.

We wandered from the house to the garden and back again with such a dogged restlessness that my mother finally told us to go and do *something*. Emma was edgy and impatient. Claudio was away a lot at this time at an editing studio in town, finishing up final work on his documentary.

We flicked through magazines, talking about nothing. I wished that Alice wasn't there; she irritated me suddenly, like an itch in my body that wouldn't go away and that I didn't understand. 'Let's go down to the creek,' I said.

I think now I simply didn't know how to be with anyone who wasn't Lizzie.

It had been raining, and the creek was muddy and swift-flowing. We waded into the water. It was icy and delicious; I felt the water should have been coloured blue, not brown. Silt had washed down in the recent rains, and lay soft and silken between my toes. I reached down and picked up a handful of it and smeared it on my arm. It smelled faintly of rotting vegetation, a smell that I have always liked.

We took off our clothes down to our knickers and submerged ourselves in the water and then stood up again, water streaming from our hair. I tried not to look at Alice because I knew she might not like me to stare; her new breasts were even tinier than mine. I reached down and took some mud from the bottom of the creek and smeared it quickly over my breasts, to cover them. Then without thinking I took another handful, and tossed it at Alice. Alice tossed a handful back at me.

Soon we were covered in mud. I stood savouring the warmth of the sun, and the sensation of the mud firming into a second skin. Without washing it off, I climbed up onto the grassy bank. Alice followed me, and we lay back, our faces turned up to the sun.

When I was so dazed by sun that I was almost asleep, I rolled sideways, and accidentally bumped into Alice. She returned the bump. We giggled, and made it into a game, rolling and bumping against each other. My eyes were dazzled by pinpricks of sunlight through my lashes.

I did a particularly vigorous roll, and felt myself come to rest partly on top of Alice. I stopped. I could feel the softness of her breast against my skin.

When I opened my eyes I saw her looking back at me.

Without thinking I put my mouth against her mouth. It wasn't a kiss, not what I'd seen Claudio and Emma do, not what I'd seen on television. With my eyes shut I licked Alice on the lips, and felt Alice's tongue touch mine. My mouth on hers was like a butterfly alighting on the edge of a puddle to drink, the lightest of touches. *Sip, sip, sip.*

My tongue went further. The inside of Alice's mouth was soft. For a moment my whole world was the warmth of the sun and the soft inside of Alice's mouth.

And then that itch I had felt with Alice earlier returned and I took Alice's bottom lip gently between my teeth. I don't know why, but very quickly and cleanly and suddenly, I bit into it. Alice cried out and pulled away, and I tasted the salt of blood.

Alice stumbled to the creek and plunged in. She rubbed at the mud on her body, trying to clean it all off. At last she emerged and stood with water streaming over her, her finger held gingerly to the sore spot on her mouth.

I saw the look of loathing on Alice's face. She said to me, slowly and emphatically, 'I am never speaking to you again. You're dirty. You're horrible. I'm going to ring my mother to come and get me.'

We didn't speak to each other again.

I stood in the driveway with her while she waited for her mother to pick her up, but she wouldn't even look at me. After the car had gone, I pulled on my comforting red beanie which smelt so strongly of myself and dragged out an old bicycle that Lizzie and I took turns on sometimes, and went for a ride. I rode and rode till I was breathless and my legs hurt, right to the top of the hill near our place. And then I turned round to go back.

It was a windy day, and as I headed down the hill I could hear the wind and feel it pushing behind me. I pedalled faster and faster, hanging on tight as I jolted through potholes and then pedalling even faster afterwards. And the wind was with me and the trees beside the road were tossing about and I became aware that I couldn't hear the wind any longer at all: I was going as fast as the wind and there was absolutely no sound, just the trees tossing and my front wheel going so fast it was blurred and my hands gripping the handlebars tight.

And then my red beanie blew off! And the wind whipped it away. All in a split second. And I didn't care, I didn't care at all.

I hadn't told Alice I was sorry, because I wasn't. I didn't feel horrible, or dirty from what I had done. I felt wonderful.

I was thirteen. My life, which I'd feared would be ordinary, had proved to be full of wonders, and I expected that more would come to me in the future.

I'd witnessed a bat draw its last breath. I'd seen my sister, in the moonlight, lift up her voice in song. A red butterfly had blossomed from my own body. I had ridden as fast as the wind.

I had drawn blood with my first kiss.

The Leather Woman

W HEN I think of the secrets of my childhood, I imagine
them as the red hibiscus flowers that grew in our garden.
They were single, dark red flowers, not the flounced double
variety; plain red flowers with an ornate gold stamen.

My mother ate those flowers. Sometimes she slipped
them into a salad for all of us; she said they were packed
with the kind of nutrients especially needed by women for
menstruation and 'women's problems'. Once I saw her
standing gazing out to where the sea lay like a string on
the horizon, slowly devouring one of the red flowers, petal
by petal, finally eating the thick, gold stamen, covered with
its down of pollen, as dusty as a moth's wing.

❧

When our parents separated, they told us about it together. But I don't think my father wanted to be there; I imagine he'd have preferred to slide out of our lives.

Stella had come to live on the north coast with Paris; she'd been waitressing at Byron Bay and had not come to see us.

Then my mother found out that Claudio had been 'seeing' Stella, which was the way she put it to us. We knew what that meant. My mother told him to leave.

They gathered us together in the living room. Lizzie and I had had an inkling of what it was all about, but Chloe did not. She was lying, half-naked, on a corduroy beanbag with her thumb in her mouth, and when Claudio said that he was moving into a house in Mullumbimby with Stella and Paris, she sat up and protested.

'But why?' she said. 'Why are you going to live with *them*?'

She drew her own conclusions. 'You love them more than us!' she said, and started to cry.

I knelt beside her and took her in my arms; her back was sweaty and covered in lint from the chair. But she pushed me away and got to her feet. She stood in front of Claudio.

'I'll still be your father, and I'll always love you,' he told her. His face said that he resented having to have this scene.

'*How* can you love them more than us?' Chloe asked. She hit him with her fist, again and again and again.

He flinched, and took the blows as if he deserved them.

'Emma and I will still be friends,' he said.

I looked at my mother's face and knew that he lied.

And then Chloe asked my parents to kiss each other.

Emma made no move towards Claudio, but kept her eyes cast to the floor. Claudio, not looking at anyone, kissed her quickly on the cheek.

❧

I wished I still had my red beanie so I could pull it down over my face and lose myself in its comforting smell. I missed my father. I missed his exuberance, the way he would catch me up in an unexpected hug. I forgot his moods and rages and sudden brooding silences.

Our mother didn't cry in front of us. But did she think we didn't see her weeping at the kitchen sink when she pretended to be washing up, or hunched over with pain as she worked in the garden? She did what women are good at doing: she put on a brave front. But her silence was stifling her. I could see it sitting like a stone in her chest. I heard her in the night vomiting up whatever little she had eaten; she couldn't stomach anything any more. In the morning she was always pale and calm, sitting in the kitchen with a cup of tea steaming in front of her.

She threw herself into gardening. She slashed and pulled and planted, coming inside with dirt under her fingernails and lantana in her hair and scratches all over her limbs. In that country, weeds grew rampant and gardening was anything but genteel.

She began to cultivate herbs. With their soft foliage and

shy flowers, they were an antidote to the headlong growth of the rainforest that surrounded the house. She favoured the nightshades, for their names and associations and often poisonous properties: henbane and belladonna and the fabulous datura, whose huge trumpets (not shy, these flowers) are borne upon a tree. Angels' trumpets, they are called, and they can give hallucinations, and kill.

Henbane she loved because the name made her laugh – she said why anyone would want to poison hens was beyond her, as hens are the most domestic and benign of birds (though perhaps it reminded her, savagely, of Stella, surrounded by all that poultry during her childhood). In the Middle Ages henbane was employed in witchcraft to cause insanity and convulsions, and to give visions – it deranged the senses of whoever took it.

And there's belladonna (*bell-a-don-na* – say it with a lilt), meaning beautiful lady, for drops of it in the eyes cause the pupils to dilate, simulating sexual arousal, and enhancing their beauty.

And there was heartsease, and love vine and love-lies-bleeding, forget-me-nots and rosemary, bitter herb, and rue. Plants for weakness of the heart, to expel pain and torments, or to aid the memory (though I would have thought that if you were in such torment, the best thing to do would be simply to forget), and motherwort, 'to help women in sore travail': all of these she grew, but they didn't seem to help, for she grew sadder and sadder.

She went to her tumbledown studio and worked at her

paintings, but nothing she did allowed her to forget.

Her friends rallied round. One of them, Edith, brought her some clay, thinking that making a sculpture from such earthy material might help. Edith made vessels on a wheel, distorting their regular shapes afterwards by pushing at them or tapping them with a paddle. She sometimes pressed her thumbs into the soft clay in secret and subtle places so that if you looked carefully you could see the mark of a human making.

Emma found that one pug of clay wasn't enough. She bought more and created a sculpture. It was life-sized, of a woman lying on her side, one leg drawn up like a sprinter's. She was slipping out of an old, wrinkled skin with a smile of triumph on her face. I asked what the sculpture meant, and my mother replied that she'd come to realise that you grow older around an unchanged core, that the young self is still there, always.

Emma's sculpture, because it was so large, took a long time to dry out, and she called it her leather woman, because at a certain stage of drying clay gets a sheen on it, like leather.

The leather woman lived on a length of plastic laid out on the floor of her workshop. We got used to stepping around her. She looked so real that I began to imagine that she could come alive. There was so much possibility in those arched feet, poised as if to leap into the world, such elasticity and power in those muscled legs.

❧

Mullumbimby is a small town overlooked by a single triangular mountain nearby and wild rainforested ranges further west. It is dead flat, with a grid of streets lined by wooden houses. At the back of the houses is a network of narrow lanes, with timber fences collapsing under the extravagance of the vines sprawling over them. It is a prodigal town, blessed by an abundance of vegetation, a place where flowers and fruit grow lavish in neglected back yards, and lie squandered and overripe and spent at the end of summer.

Claudio wanted us children to come and stay with him in the house they'd rented there. Lizzie didn't want to go, saying to me under her breath, 'He's not even my father.' But she agreed finally for my sake, and our mother's.

In the old house near the river I wandered through the afternoon-darkened rooms when everyone else was out. I enjoyed the temporary feel of the place. The telephone sat on the floor in an empty room; boxes of stuff sat randomly about. The unpolished timber floors echoed when you walked on them. The house had no need of blinds, for trees surrounded it, trees covered in morning-glory vines with their purple flowers. Looking through those windows was like peering at a stage set draped with tattered green curtains, through which crept the small brown river at the end of the back yard. You could smell the silt from the river, and it reminded me of Alice, and mud, and the taste of blood.

Paris hadn't changed much. She still had that same sharp and considering look. She glanced up from her homework at the kitchen table on that first afternoon and said, 'Hello,' in a way that told me that she didn't much care whether I liked her or not.

I was pleased to see that Stella wasn't much of a cook. We had vegetarian sausages and vegetables that first night, and the sausages were smooth and pale, like creatures that had never seen the sun, the vegetables lumpy or mushy, under- or over-cooked. Claudio hadn't helped cook, of course; he rarely did. He sat in the bare room with the telephone and 'did business' until dinnertime.

Paris speared a sausage with her fork and held it up in front of her face to examine it. 'Pooh!' she said, and started to nibble it from one end, still holding it on her fork.

'Pooh!' said Chloe, laughing, holding up her sausage in imitation.

'Are you still playing the guitar?' Stella asked Lizzie.

'Of course.'

'It's her passion,' I started to explain, but Lizzie gave me such a look that I shut up at once. *'Be mine tonight!'* sang Claudio. He had opened a bottle of wine and was steadily working his way through it without Stella's help. He'd given us all a little, just a taste in the bottom of a glass. Lizzie ignored hers, while Paris tipped her own few drops down her throat immediately and then sent her hand out stealthily across the table towards Lizzie's glass. I sipped carefully; the wine tasted of rich, red moths that had drowned in a vat of grapes, and then been strained through a cloth that had lain on a dusty road for some time.

Paris closed her eyes and reached her tongue to the

bottom of Lizzie's glass and lapped at it. 'Mmmm. A nice little drop!' she said.

Claudio helped Lizzie and me with the washing-up afterwards. Lizzie was silent. She refused to look at him. 'Oh, Lizzie, Lizzie, Lizzie,' he said, ruefully, trying to jolly her along, putting on one of his broad smiles that showed his front teeth almost fiercely. (My father's face was always prepared for people, he was always aware of the effect he was having on others. I have seldom seen him with his face bare, not readied to receive someone's gaze. Sometimes I think that all that self-conscious readiness must have worn him out.)

'Oh, Claudio, Claudio, Claudio!' said Lizzie, her hand over her heart, not smiling, still not looking at him. She flicked the tea towel at him and left the room.

I found her later, staring out the window of our empty, threadbare room, a room like a blank slate that no one cared to scribble on. She had thrown the window open and stood with her arms braced on the timber frame. Outside was black.

We lay in the dark and couldn't sleep; I heard Lizzie tossing and turning. Our mattresses were on the floor, and although it wasn't cold, Stella had come in with extra bedding. 'There's a mist that comes in from the river sometimes,' she said.

I lay in my strange bed and stretched luxuriously. I didn't mind the strangeness of it; there was the feeling of possibilities. My body felt strong; I felt power coil right through it like a spring, waiting to be released. I wasn't tired at all: I wanted to *do* something.

༄

I imagined the leather woman lying in my mother's workshop.

Moonlight comes through the window and falls onto her. She stirs and shifts about impatiently, casting off the old wrinkled skin as if it is a blanket she has no use for. She pauses, her eyes alert and alive.

With the grace of a sprinter at a starting block she rises in one swift movement from the floor, goes to the door, and opens it. She stands with her head held high as if listening, then leaves quickly without a backward glance. She runs down the road through the trees, and her legs make a cracking sound like a whip that carries far into the night. She passes farmhouses, and dogs bark as she goes by. Her path can be traced by the cries of *Shaddup, you bastards!* that follow her all the way through the countryside, and the lights shooting on and then off again as the commotion dies down. At last she comes to the outskirts of town, and under a streetlight she sits, sinewy, naked, expectant, on the rail of a cattle yard.

༄

Sound came from Claudio and Stella's room down the hallway, and Lizzie sat up sharply. 'Oh, God, I can't listen to that! Come on!'

She pulled on her clothes. 'Oh, come on, Laura, we don't have to lie here listening to them fucking all night.'

I dressed and, on feet as poised for flight as the leather woman's, we went down the long wooden steps at the back of the house and were free.

Just down the road was an old house painted white, with white marble statues in the yard: children in classical poses, with white, unseeing eyes. Tendrils of climbing plants caught at their ankles and wound their way up their legs, whispering to them, *caught you, caught you, caught you.*

We walked quickly, our eyes avid, peering through leafy front yards to where television sets flickered. We heard the steps of heavy-footed people sounding on timber floors. A dusky cat sat on a fence post but fled as we approached. I felt powerful and vigorous, with the whole town of Mullumbimby at our feet. There was mist, and we revelled in the glory of it, at being out when we should have been in bed. I felt so complete and strong and alive that I flung my arms round Lizzie and kissed her full on the mouth. She pushed me away, laughing, and we danced through the streets, utterly enchanted by the night – simply by the night and the amazement of being alive.

We slowed down to smell a rose that leaned over a fence; it was black in the night but still smelled like a rose. But overlaying that odour I thought I could smell the dark rankness of river mud, and hear the sound of the leather woman coming closer as she strode through the streets, her legs as supple as ribbons, looking for us.

Then I saw a figure halt in the shadow of a tree behind us. It was Paris. The streetlight revealed her face as she moved out of the shadow.

'What are you doing?'

'Following you!'

She hadn't bothered to dress, and was wearing pyjamas with teacups all over them. They were too big for her and hung over her wrists. Her feet were bare, and the cuffs of the pyjama pants had splashes of mud on them where she had gone through puddles.

'You'd better join us,' said Lizzie, authoritative and grown-up. She held out her hand, but Paris didn't take it. She walked close behind us, averting her gaze, pretending she was on her own. When we found ourselves unexpectedly back at our own front gate there seemed nothing to do but to go in. We crept up the steps and inside. We had said not another word to Paris and quietly she made her way to her room, as we did.

The house was as silent as a damp old wooden house could be. It made vague, soft, complaining noises. In the kitchen there were secret scurryings of cockroaches and the flap of moths against the windows. Before I went to sleep I sensed that the leather woman had found her way to the house. She went down the hallway to Claudio and Stella's room and stood looking at them sleeping for a long time.

∾

Claudio and Stella took us all to the beach, often. We were

used to going with Claudio and Emma, of course, and we noticed the differences when Stella was there.

Our mother used to avoid the hot part of the day, and she seldom swam. Emma went to the beach to walk and to think and to gaze out to sea, getting ideas for paintings.

Stella liked to go when the sun blazed, so she could sunbake. She would lie on a towel reading a novel and smoking a cigarette, her eyes squinted. She wore nothing but a G-string and became browner and browner. When she walked down to the water to cool off, she was noticeably lean and brown and naked.

'I *refuse* to look,' Lizzie hissed at me, narrowing her eyes in disgust. We took ourselves off up the beach with Chloe.

Chloe had a mania for collecting things, now. One day she found scores of little fish with boxy shapes that looked utterly surprised to find themselves washed up on the shore, dead, and she took home every one of them. She found shellfish with the insides not yet rotted away, and seahorses, and seaweed like necklaces. All of it stank, and she put it under the house in Mullumbimby, saying that the smell would go away one day.

There had been a bushfire a couple of kilometres up the coast, and we arrived on one scorchingly hot day to find ash in the water, and burnt leaves all along the tideline. Along with the leaves were cicadas, burnt black, and hundreds of Christmas beetles, still shiny. Chloe and I walked together, she with her head bent low, searching for any sign of life.

She stopped. 'I can hear a fizzing noise. Listen.'

Crouching down, she said, 'This beetle is moving. It's hissing.'

Stranded all along the beach we found, when we looked closely, dozens of live Christmas beetles. Somehow they had survived the fire, been blown out to sea on the debris, and floated back in again on the tide. One was still clinging to the gumleaf it had coasted in to shore on, like a miniature board-rider.

Chloe made me and Lizzie and Paris help her pick them up. Each of us loaded them onto the palm of one hand, and all the way up the soft underside of our arms to the elbow; once they were there they started to creep about. 'Stop tickling!' Chloe commanded them, giggling. We carried them carefully up to the dunes where there were trees to deposit them on. Some beetles put out their legs to take hold of a twig, but some were unable to grasp a foothold and fell to the ground. A few of them took off from our outstretched arms before we even got to the dunes. We stopped and gazed up at them as they soared above us.

ᏺ

Lizzie and I went out in the night again and again. We were the waltzers down damp footpaths, the midnight ramblers who prowled the streets witnessing everything. We heard voices raised in argument, or soft words of love from front verandahs. There were occasional fellow revellers of the night – people who dined in their gardens with the soft light of candles; we heard their intimate laughter and talk and the clink of glasses and cutlery. There were lone people who squatted on their front steps smoking a cigarette or hugging their knees to their chest – people like us, who knew the attraction of darkness.

'*Did ya hear about the midnight rambler,*' Lizzie sang. Her voice was wistful and shy in the dark, a bit off-key, a bit unsure of itself. I wished she'd sing louder, and longer. Our ramblings were mostly accompanied by the muffled dialogue of television programs. There was the occasional plinking of a guitar, and then Lizzie paused to listen, her face still with longing.

Sometimes we abandoned the streets of wooden houses for the mystery of the park near the river where rainforest trees breathed out an odour of glossy green, and canna lilies, which had been red in the daylight, stood with black spears massed like a waiting army.

Paris always followed. '*I'm a nuisance, I'm a nuisance,*' she sang under her breath. We allowed her to catch us up. Lizzie stood, hands on hips. 'You may as well walk *with* us!'

I knew the leather woman followed us too. She knew every useful shadow; she practised the art of pausing and blending with her surroundings at exactly the right moment. I never really thought of us as being out alone.

Once, when we passed a cottage almost entirely concealed by trees, Lizzie said, 'There's Al's place.' She ducked up the front path and pushed her way among foliage at the side of the house to where light shone out from a window.

Paris and I followed, and the three of us stood at the lighted window and peered in.

Al was the person Lizzie spent most of her time with at school. He wasn't her boyfriend, she said. He was in his room, perched on his bed reading, surrounded by the hundreds of books he collected for next to nothing from op shops. He looked up, bemused at the faces peering unexpectedly through his window so late. We were standing on the raised brick edge of a garden bed, so we teetered a bit, except for Lizzie, who was tall enough to stand on the ground.

Al smiled and came to the window. He was pale and thin and freckled. 'What are *you* all doing?' he whispered.

'Oh, just walking, you know,' said Lizzie, and grinned back at him. 'Bye!'

We kept going. There was no need to talk. There was just the shared pleasure of being out of our beds when we were meant to be asleep, and of the wonder and mystery of the dark. It was a guilty pleasure but we were unrepentant.

The leather woman came into the house when we were finally all in bed. She came unsurely at first, and then boldly, as if she owned the place. She listened outside the bedroom of Claudio and Stella, and she watched over Chloe, who slept soundly with her plump arms flung out behind her head and never stirred when the rest of us went out. She even watched over Lizzie and me for a time, pleased that we were safely back at last.

If I woke in the night I always knew that she had been

there. There was a sense of departure in our room, a distur-
bance in the molecules of the air, a faint whiff of clay.

༻

Guiltily, I began to enjoy staying in my father's house. It
wasn't simply the freedom of the night walks. It was the care-
lessness of the household, the sense that it was all temporary, that what you did there didn't matter as much as it
did at home. It was like being on holiday. I began to like
all those unpacked boxes, the scrappiness of the kitchen,
the starkness of the bare boards and the odd bits of furniture placed just anyhow.

Guiltily, treacherously, I arrived each week at Claudio's
house with a sense of release from the sadness that pervaded
my mother's life. We had different rituals and habits there.
Lizzie and I sat on the front steps with our elbows on our
knees and stared out at the street, enjoying the atmosphere
of having people around. It was a street of musicians, and
we listened to the ragged sounds of the jazz band that practised two doors down.

Alice walked past on the other side of the street on the
way to a music lesson, her flute case in her hand, studiously
not looking in our direction. She stared down at her bare
feet and walked gracefully, as slender as a sardine in flared
slacks, her bare belly stuck slightly forward. A little while
later she walked past again in the opposite direction.

The band was still playing, and we tapped our feet to the
beat, enjoying the untidy sound, the stopping and starting

as they tried to perfect it. An old woman sweeping her path saw us and screwed up her face and put her hands over her ears as if she couldn't stand the noise. Then she grinned and took her hands down and put them on her hips, moving from side to side. 'Oo, Oo, I feel like dancing!' she said. Lizzie smiled at her and leapt down the steps to check the letter-box, leaning quickly over the front fence and looking all the way down the street. No one ever wrote her a letter but Lizzie thought there might be something interesting there one day. She also held out hope that a fascinating person would suddenly materialise. In a town, with people always about, all things are possible.

I liked to think so too. Mullumbimby swarmed with girls with bare brown arms and midriffs and flirtatious smiles. I would dream for days about the softness of a neck or the shape of a mouth; I imagined seizing some stranger's hand and biting her playfully on her shoulder and running away before she had time to be indignant about it. But of course I told no one of this and I kept apart from the girls at school. There were girls there who would thump you if they didn't like your hairstyle.

Lizzie and I took pleasure in everything. We laughed at nothing, or everything, rolling about on the floor of our bare room. A single word was enough to set us off. We bought packets of chocolate mint biscuits and ate the lot at once, peeling off layers of mint cream and squashing it greedily into our mouths. Fortified by sugar, we began to speculate about the things that still puzzled us.

'Mum's sister who died . . .' I'd say.

'Drowned . . .' Lizzie would correct.

The thought of drowning, of submerging for ever, was such a final surrender that I shivered. 'I wonder why Mum never talks about her at all? I'd talk about *you*.'

And we wondered about Lizzie's father. 'Maybe you should *ask* her. Now you're older . . .' I suggested. But Lizzie jumped up and went to the window.

'Look at Paris,' she said. 'Making spells, I bet.'

❧

Paris, in the wild garden, picks absent-mindedly at the scab on her elbow and assembles a collection of ingredients for her magic potion: three leaves from a sandpaper fig, four seeds from a black-bean tree – though she couldn't have named either – and two black and white magpie feathers. She sings to herself and looks around for something else that might be magical and finds a seahorse that Chloe has brought back from the beach and left to dry out under the house. It smells suitably potent.

'What are you doing?' says Stella, coming down from the laundry with a basket of washing.

'Nothing, nothing, nothing . . .' sings Paris, skipping out of her way with a private smile on her face. She spins round with a flourish, wriggling her fingers. 'Making *magic*!' she says, and disappears up the side of the house.

By the time she comes back, Stella has hung out the washing and departed again. Paris assembles the ingredients for her spell in a pattern on the ground and murmurs an incantation over them:

I want a sister, a sister, a sister . . .

&

If I haven't said much about Claudio and Stella, it is because we were indifferent to them. Not entirely indifferent: I think Lizzie and I wanted both to know and not know what the adults were up to. Do I contradict myself?

But we were too immersed in our immediate world to be bothered with them. We were grand and callous and selfish and self-absorbed as children are, caught up with the immediacy of the smell of roses and the taste of chocolate, the trivial, engrossing, delicious details that made up our lives.

&

And yet I was aware of how our mother was filled with grief and jealousy.

&

It eats her up. Her love for Claudio is a great Rasputin of a love, dark and bearded and vile. It comes to her in the dead of night with rank, lustful breath and mad eyes and she stumbles out to the garden and rubs dirt and leaves into her face and hair. Her love won't die. She has tried to forget him. She has shot her love for him in the back ten times, but still it staggers to its feet. She has buried it alive, but still a great hoary hand breaks through the soil and comes to seize her by the throat.

&

After a while Emma's sculpture, the leather woman, dried out completely. Her body became dusty and lifeless. To look as good as her old leather-hard self, she would have to be glazed and fired. But then she would be a glazed woman, Emma said, a glass woman. Not plastic, as soft clay is, but brittle. Besides, we didn't have a kiln large enough to fire her in.

One day I helped my mother drag the leather woman outside on her plastic sheet. She lay underneath the trees, and over time, rain fell on her and blunted the detail of her features. Leaves fell on her and began to conceal her naked-ness. She was on the way to going back into the earth.

And only then did I stop seeing the woman who stood in the shadows across the street when she thought everyone was asleep, watching the house, her eyes dark hollows of grief.

Goblin Market

Lizzie makes her way through the Saturday market in the park, treading as carefully and fastidiously as a cat. She does not yet know she is beautiful, but she sees people look at her, and keep looking, especially men. They must register her size, she thinks: she towers above most people. Lizzie is tall and long-legged and undainty, and she feels painfully the scrutiny of others. She wears her hair in a thick gold plait; it draws too much attention to her if she wears it loose.

It seems to her that this is a market full of people who look like animals: English animals from the picture books of her childhood. That man there selling jewellery, with the small eyes and pinched mouth, is a rat; and the man making coffee, who has black and grey hair brushed back in a wave from his forehead, is a badger.

And she can't help noticing that there are a number of dainty mice, almost an infestation of them – the woman selling fairy wings and dresses, for example, and the one at the plant stall wearing overalls, and the girl walking by clutching her boyfriend's hand as if she's afraid he'll escape from her. They are small women, with small, pointed, pretty faces.

The market is achingly full of luscious food. Lizzie has a large person's appetite, and food attracts her. Watermelons and mangoes, strawberries, rockmelons and pineapples, all call to her in high, fruit-like voices, saying, 'Eat me, Lizzie, eat me!'

She buys a large fruit salad served in half a scooped-out pineapple with a mound of whipped cream on top, and finds a quiet corner of the market to stop and eat it in. Food is to be savoured and appreciated, she feels, and shouldn't be eaten walking about, or when one's attention is focused on something else.

She finds herself near a stall where a man in a top-hat made of satin patches is selling coloured balls for juggling. He stands out the front and juggles as if he doesn't care whether people buy or not, and despite herself, Lizzie finds herself watching him as she eats; her eye is drawn to him again and again. He has an attractively ugly face. He looks like a hound, with his loose, baggy jowls; his whole face is baggy and wrinkled.

One of the balls seems to slip out of his hands accidentally, though Lizzie doesn't see how it could have, and it lands
at Lizzie's feet. With a grin, he skips over to her and says,
'Sorry about that,' picking it up with a deft swoop, but he
doesn't seem sorry at all. 'Give me a bite of your fruit salad,
love.' Lizzie looks at him haughtily and decides he is a
goblin. He is easily as old as Claudio, and smaller than she
is. The crown of his hat is ridiculously high, it is a joke
top-hat, and it is as baggy and pouched as his face is.

'Oh well, don't, then,' he says, shrugging in an exaggerated fashion, going back to his stall.

Lizzie can't help stealing another look at his remarkable
face. It is a landscape of changing expression and appears
never to be still: the folds are constantly shifting and refig-
uring. There seems to be more skin on his face than there
needs to be, and it doesn't know where to go.

She sees him again later that afternoon at the poets' cafe
in town. Lizzie doesn't want to go home, or rather, back to
the house that Claudio and Stella share, where she's meant
to be staying this weekend. So she loiters, finds things to do,
places to hang out. The poets' cafe is as good as any.

The goblin man is still wearing his hat; he's sitting with
some young women at a table at the front near the microphone. The women have that air of lush insouciance that
Lizzie both despises and envies. They wear skimpy tops
made of embroidered satin that reveal the shape of their
breasts, skirts that flow over their backsides and hips like
water, clothes that wouldn't look out of place in a bordello.

Or so she thinks. She has heard the word and has only an inkling of what it means.

She watches the performers. Women get up and declaim the words they've strung together so boldly and unashamedly that Lizzie wants to blush with embarrassment for them, they are so pleased with their banality. A man goes to the front with an acoustic guitar and strums it while he recites, and Lizzie thinks hotly, *I can play better than that.* He holds the guitar as if it is of no consequence, and his words make no sense to her.

There is a man in the corner with a face like a toad, and another one looks like a large-eared fox. A girl with a close-shaven head and a ring through her nose swaddles a mauve shawl around herself like the wings of a bat at rest. Lizzie leans forward and takes a long sip of her orange juice, shutting out the sight of them. The whole place is a menagerie.

But then she looks up, only to see the goblin man turn from whispering to one of his women friends to give Lizzie a grin, as if he's known she was there all the time and has deliberately decided to acknowledge her. She stares back, her face unmoving, and he gets up and walks over to her, swaggering, grinning at her. He takes a business card from his top pocket and presents it to her. 'I think we should get acquainted.'

Lizzie glances at the card. *Tom Roberts, Poet and Healer* says the card boastfully, with an address and phone number. Lizzie stares ahead and pushes the card into the slick of water that her icy glass has left on the table. 'Come and see me some time,' says the goblin man. He winks and returns to his table at the front.

A girl comes in with a carpet snake draped around her shoulders. Heads turn, but she pretends not to notice. She makes her way languidly to the front of the cafe and to the goblin man's table. She has knowing, slanted eyes, and she fondles the snake absently as she speaks to him. Then she draws up a chair and sits down, and the goblin man reaches round her shoulder and gives her a squeeze. And all this time the snake is draped passively around her. It is unusually sluggish – is it blind, or drugged, or sick? Lizzie watches, horrified that a snake, a wild creature that should be free, is being worn like just another accessory.

Lizzie can't tear her gaze away from the snake girl's bare back, revealed by a halter top. Her dark, frizzy hair comes halfway down it, and the goblin man is tracing a pattern lightly over her skin, again and again and again, the lightest of touches; Lizzie wants to scream with irritation, for she can feel her own skin crawling. The snake girl pays him no attention at all; it is as if nothing is happening to her, but she doesn't move away either. She is as passive as the snake.

Then the goblin man (Tom Roberts, Poet and Healer!) goes to the microphone. He grins and stands there in his ridiculous hat. 'I am going to recite a love poem,' he says, and he begins, but it is so disgusting that Lizzie's fingers twitch, and, unconsciously gripping the card he has given her, flicking and bending it in annoyance, she scrapes her chair back and leaves without looking back, leaves the whole lot of them, the snake girl, the fox, the toad, and the goblin man, whose words follow her, and seem to trail behind her all the way down the street.

&

That evening, late, Lizzie cranks up her amp to its loudest. She lets the notes rip through the night. She wants distortion and feedback and out-and-out destruction. She can feel the music bouncing through her chest as she plays, rippling up and down her body; she plays angrily and broods on her knowledge that to be a girl is to be faced irrevocably with your own unimportance. For in truth Lizzie wants to play like Jimi Hendrix; she wants to *be* Jimi Hendrix, but she is only a sweet young girl with a long fair plait and legs that people always stare at. She's a girl, she's white, she comes from Mullumbimby, and she knows she stands not a hope in the world of anyone taking her or her music seriously.

And now Claudio comes roaring and bellowing into the room, and demands that she *turn the bloody thing off*, and Lizzie rips the cord from the amp and, carrying her guitar as it is, cord dangling uselessly, she heads out into the night.

She left the house on impulse but knows she'll find refuge at Al's place, so she strides confidently along the dark streets. Al is Lizzie's only real friend. She doesn't like girls, not really; they don't share her passion. She and Al have nothing in common either, apart from obsession itself (hers for guitars, Al's for books) and a certainty of their own strangeness and apartness from everyone else.

Al looks up as she appears at his window and does his startled movement, elbows flying everywhere and shoulders twitching. But he manages to get to his feet and, without saying a word, Lizzie hands the guitar through to him and clambers in after it.

'Can I stay the night?' It's a demand, not a question. Lizzie looks around her. 'Don't you have a spare bed?'

Since she's been to his house innumerable times, she should know that he doesn't, but Lizzie's not good at noticing such things. They stay up a while longer, Al reading a thick volume of the collected plays of William Shakespeare and Lizzie plinking quietly at her guitar. Al haunts places that sell old books and has collected enough reading matter for a lifetime. He buys books on anything as long as they're cheap: the rules of tennis, which he doesn't play, and fairy tales, and Euclidian geometry. Lizzie thinks he buys them for the titles, sometimes, or the smell, for he certainly doesn't read them all. She suspects that he simply likes the word *Euclidian*, that it holds some magical promise for him; she feels that way about particular combinations of notes, though she's never actually put them into a tune.

When he's absorbed in a book his usually ugly face takes on a kind of beauty, and Lizzie, at those times, loves him more than anyone in the world. *He's a genius*, she thinks, admiringly, as she strums her guitar softly. Without an amp, her electric guitar sounds like an insect lost in the bottom of a box and searching for a way out. She thinks of the glory of the music she made earlier, when the notes of her guitar tore through the night and stung Claudio into a rage.

Eventually they get into Al's bed, Lizzie's head at the top, Al's at the bottom. Lizzie slides in next to Al's pale, thin body. His feet are endearingly like a pair of scaled fish next to her face, and she lies awake for a long time, staring at the shape of her guitar, which seems naked and vulnerable propped there without its protective case. She thinks of the snake girl and the goblin man, and how her skin would erupt with irritation, if anyone were to touch her like that.

やく

'Lizzie stayed the night,' Al tells his mother the next morning. 'But you don't need to worry, nothing happened.'

Al's mother spends her days in bed. Mostly she sleeps. She has slept and slept since they ran away from his father two years ago. Al is pleased they left, because the violence that was once part of their lives has also gone. But he worries about her and her inability to do anything any more.

He looks after her tenderly. He brings her cups of tea, and food, though he often finds the tea still in the cup and cold, the food congealed. He takes the ATM card from her purse and shops for them and pays the rent. Some of his own student allowance goes towards this too. He buys her little gifts: plastic frogs, which he has decided she collects. It's nice to have a mother with an interest. He buys her cakes of nice-smelling soap, and she smiles and puts them under her pillow. On good days she gets up and showers and he finds her in the living room reading a magazine.

In whimsical moments Al says that he is really an axolotl. That's what Al is short for, he says, it's the first and last letters of his real name. Lizzie saw him catch sight of himself in the bathroom mirror. He hissed at his reflection with narrowed eyes and made clawing motions with his hands. Now he and Lizzie sit together on the back step eating toast and honey in the morning sunshine, Al with his long body stretched out. 'Warming myself up on my rock,' he says, 'so I can get going for the day.'

Al sees himself as lizard-like and unattractive. He has a long, pale body, a freckled face, and strong, sandy hairs sprouting from his legs. But Lizzie sees the beauty in him. There is a sensuality in Al of a kind that Lizzie recognises, for she's noticed it in herself, a sensuality that has nothing to do with another person, or love, or sex, just with the pleasure of responding to the world.

But lately, certain things have disturbed her, such as the goblin man stroking the girl's bare back at the poetry cafe. And she remembers that first night she and Laura went out to walk in the dark, how Laura took hold of her and unexpectedly kissed her. Her sister's mouth, soft and childish and innocent, was so unexpected and lovely that she wipes her mouth with the back of her hand at the memory.

'So,' says Al, sitting up and stretching. 'What happened last night?'

Lizzie shakes her head. 'I don't know. Some stupid fight with Claudio.'

Al squeezes his eyes shut and lifts his pale face to the sun with a smile so that it is like a flower unfolding. 'I don't mind you coming over,' he says, 'but if you do it too often, I'll need another bed.'

&

Lizzie has something hidden. Something under her shirt. A secret wound. A piercing. Her bellybutton now has a slim gold ring inserted in it, and it gently weeps and festers. This pleases Lizzie, for she has always felt a hurt somewhere about herself and now it has been made manifest.

She has found that pain can be exquisite, a secret knowledge that sustains you. Lizzie has grown fond of her wound. She examines it briefly in the washroom at school and applies more ointment and goes off to console herself with her guitar.

&

At a loose end, she discovers the goblin man's card in the bottom of her bag. It is as creased and crinkled as his face. *Tom Roberts, Poet and Healer*, it says.

The house is a small timber cottage in the tail end of one of the shopping streets. Lizzie pauses and takes in the peeling paintwork and the tattered Indian flag that serves as a curtain in the front window before striding up the front path between yellowing palm trees. A frangipani has dropped fragrant pink flowers onto the ground and she feels their fleshiness beneath the thin soles of her sandals. The door is open and Lizzie knocks. She feels no nervousness as she hears footsteps responding; she feels not even curiosity, just a strange kind of anger and a power she's never felt before.

When he comes to the door, she refuses to register the speculative look on his face; she simply stands without speaking and lets him say, 'Well . . .' and then, 'Come in . . .'

She follows him down a hallway with small darkened rooms on either side. At the rear of the house is a long enclosed verandah with a kitchen at one end. He motions her to a battered couch, but she ignores the offer and glances dismissively towards a large painting that hangs on the end wall, so thick with paint that it almost looks like a relief sculpture.

'That's an awful waste of paint,' she says tartly.

He grins at her. 'Tea?'

They sit outside in a garden that is a tangle of greenery. Lizzie sips her tea and glances at him and finds herself looking into his eyes and responding to his wrinkled smile. She begins to feel afraid of her own impulses, and wonders what has brought her there.

Poet and Healer his card says. Perhaps she wants healing, and thinks that in some obscure way he could help.

Lizzie makes her way to Tom Roberts's house again and again. She is repelled and fascinated by him, by the way he appears to both mock and yearn for her. She grows familiar with his squat metal teapot stained with a stripe of tannin below the spout and resists the urge to clean it off. She sits on the floor in the square of morning sunlight that comes through the back door, gazing out at the garden. He has other young women visit him, she knows. Sometimes she catches the heady scent of ylang ylang oil, and fancies that bare brown feet and a jangling anklet have just whisked out the door. She learns that someone named Jamila has planted the herb garden among a radiating circle of bricks in the back yard. But it is dry and lifeless and no one waters it any longer, and she suspects that Jamila is long gone. She finds the teapot scrubbed clean one day and wonders who has cleaned it.

Sometimes other people are there, drinking coffee, smoking dope, listening to music. Tom Roberts entertains them all, he dances around playing host, his laughter bouncing round the thin timber walls. He does magic tricks, pulling coins from behind people's ears. Lizzie sees him watching her from across the room, seeming to consider her possibilities. Lizzie can bear his gaze, for she feels she's in control. She stares back, unsmiling. She doesn't want him, she doesn't even like him particularly.

Lizzie prefers it when she finds him there alone. She doesn't know what she wants from him. And what does he want from her? His look of secret triumph each time he finds her at the door troubles her. She vows each time not to come back. But she always does. She despises his scrawny chest with greying hairs and the way he gets around without a shirt. Despite his being thin, there is a bulge of flabby skin over the waistband of his jeans.

He reads his poems to her sometimes, watching her face, observing her reaction closely. She thinks his poems paltry, but stops herself from saying so. Kindness is a habit with her.

There is an ambiguous struggle going on between them. Who has the upper hand? Neither of them knows. He often looks at her with something like a leer. She affects not to notice. She emanates scorn.

'You're getting pretty, Lizzie,' he tells her one day. He playfully squeezes her waist in passing, putting his hand under her shirt. His fingers pass across the metal ring and stop there. This is the first time he has ever touched her. 'What's this, Lizzie? A pierced bellybutton? I didn't think you were the type.'

Lizzie removes his hand and adjusts her shirt. 'What type?' she says coolly. 'Is there a type?'

Later, when she collects her bag, the wordless signal that she is leaving, he brings out a jar and opens the lid. It is filled with dark liquid and squashy, shapeless objects. 'A present,' he says. 'Try one.'

She laughs. Her scorn is genuine. 'My parents ate those back in the *seventies*.'

'I'll give you some for later. A gift.' He extracts two tiny mushrooms and puts them in a plastic sandwich bag. 'Preserved in honey. What could be purer?'

He hands it to her with a flourish.

She bestows a luminous, insincere smile on him. He smiles back at her, blissfully, too eagerly, closing his eyes and savouring the moment with a sweet, sad expression on his face. It's like smiling at babies, she thinks. You don't even have to mean it and the fools always smile back.

❧

Still, she remembers the way Tom Roberts's hands have touched her, discovering her hurt, her secret wound. She remembers the feel of his roughened fingers on the soft flesh of her waist and, days later, when she sees Claudio's fingers slide inside the opening at the side of the loose overalls Stella is wearing, she walks away in disgust.

She goes to see Al. She's been neglecting him, and now she needs him.

'Can I show you something?' she asks, and without waiting for his reply she lifts her shirt to reveal the gold ring in its bed of weeping flesh.

'Lizzie!' says Al, coming over to peer at the wound through his glasses. 'Why on earth did you do that?'

❧

She becomes enthralled by food. She sits in a cafe alone, imbibing iced chocolate and carrot cake with cream cheese icing. She sucks up the sweet dark liquid, licks cream from her lips, and lets her fork fall through the soft cake. Scooping it up, she allows the cake to remain in her mouth for long moments before swallowing. Her experience is intense and private.

Food becomes her religion. She bows her head before

slicing a mango with a knife, one cheek at a time. The act is at once a submission and a sacrifice. She eats watermelon and spits the seeds slowly into the ferns, leaning over the verandah in a silent communion with the ground.

She ambushes food; she becomes a mistress of tactics. She walks casually past the fruit bowl, reaching out at the last moment to seize a banana. She takes grapes by surprise, standing under the vine lost in thought, then reaching suddenly upwards to tear away a bunch before it can antici-pate the attack. She retreats to the shrubbery to eat each grape carefully, squeezing the flesh into her puckered mouth and discarding the skins for the ants.

Her body becomes lush and full, reminiscent of the fruit and cream she feeds it with. Her breasts grow round and ripe and heavy. Her haunches are smooth and curved, plump and delicious-looking. She stands naked before the mirror and turns around to appraise them, running her fingers appreciatively over the line of her waist and hips before slipping a slinky frock over the top. Her stomach is no longer concave. It swells delicately below her bellybutton. The wound has healed and she wears clothes that expose the small gold ring and the soft mound of her belly. She surveys herself in the mirror and likes what she sees.

❧

It has come into her consciousness that you can be someone other than your dull self. You can become whoever you want to be simply by pretending. You can play-act, and it is for real. Slither out of your old skin and take on another. She studies other girls, other women. At a party, one of those flirty, flighty parties that Claudio drags them to, she sees a girl who isn't pretty but can make people believe she is. She wears a skimpy black top and a black velvet stole round her shoulders. Lizzie watches as the girl weaves between the crowd of people, watches as the girl looks lingeringly over her shoulder at no one in particular and slowly lowers the stole to reveal one plump, creamy shoulder.

Lizzie, as beautiful as the day, bites her bottom lip and holds her breath. She watches and learns. She has always bought clothes but has simply *worn* them. Now she sees that you can do more with them than that. You can become someone other.

For a time she becomes bolder and more expansive, especially when she isn't at home with her mother. In the house in Mullumbimby she flings the windows open to the night with a broad sweep of her arms, embracing the darkness. She spends long steamy sessions in the shower and then walks about the house with only a towel wrapped around her, leaning from the windows in the living room to brush out her damp hair, shaking it and letting the breeze whip it until it crackles dry. She is forever hanging out of windows, as if houses are too small to contain her. She pulls the long blonde hairs from her hairbrush and, wrapped only in a too-small towel, leans outside on tiptoes and scatters the strands to the four winds.

✌

She has grown plump and beautiful but she still wears her hair in a chaste plait. She returns to Tom Roberts's house again and again, never knowing what it is she wants. She hasn't eaten the mushrooms he's given her. He never touches her again.

✌

She wants to do something with all this ripeness. 'Kiss me,' she says to Al one day, and he complies, pressing his mouth childishly to hers. It is a strange, sexless, unerotic kiss, but it leaves them both shaken, for it has shifted the ground between them and it will take a long time for them to regard each other as they had before.

'We shouldn't have done that,' says Al, returning to his book, his neck suffused with red. 'You shouldn't do that to me, Lizzie.'

She is heartless. She leaves him and goes straight to St Vinnies, where she tries on clothes out on the open floor of the shop, ignoring the way people stare at her. She pulls on dowdy floral rayon dresses that grow instantly glamorous when they connect with her body. Frivolous net petticoats gain in stature and acquire a gravitas they've only dreamed of. Everything looks wonderful on her. Ancient unwanted clothes made from lace and satin she adds to the pile that grows on the floor. She scoops the lot up in her arms and strides to the counter and buys them all for a song.

৵

Despite her love of the freedom at Claudio's place in town, the only place she really thinks of as home is the one in the hills with her mother. There, Lizzie takes out the small plastic parcel the goblin man has given her. She sets off with it across the hot midday garden and crosses paths with Emma, who has a paintbrush in her hand, on her own quest to her studio to work. Emma spies the parcel in Lizzie's hand; Lizzie tries to conceal it, putting it behind her quickly, making it all the more obvious.

'What have you got there?' Emma's query is light and idly curious.

'Nothing.'

'You're so secretive.'

'Oh, and *you're* not!'

The exchange takes place in passing; it is over in seconds, but in a few moments the tone has changed so swiftly it leaves Lizzie reeling. She can see by the look of her mother's disappearing back how she's hurt her.

She goes to the seat that looks east over the escarpment. Unwrapping the package quickly she hesitates only a moment. The mushrooms are misshapen and in a puddle of watery grey ooze; their moisture has diluted the honey so that it is unrecognisable. She places one and then the other on her tongue and swallows quickly. They are like earthy, wet oysters.

Lizzie sits for a long time looking at the view and decides nothing is going to happen. Her stomach is faintly queasy and she wonders if she should stick her fingers down her throat and try to bring it all up.

She closes her eyes and feels the world spin. When she was a child she would make herself dizzy spinning round and round like a top and then sit on the ground and open her eyes, to find with delight that she had been able to alter reality.

She feels no such delight now. She sits down on the ground with a bump, hoping the earth will steady her. She thinks at once of her mother, and what they've just said and not said to each other.

I think I'll die from not speaking.

Red hibiscus flowers nod to her and she goes over to them, willing them to speak. She plucks one and laps at the red petals with her tongue. Red for danger, red for rage, red for sex.

The petals are veined like flesh but as fine as skin. They give way beneath her teeth; she savours the texture and gulps them down, and then begins on the yellow stamens, which are thicker and harder to swallow. The red of the petals is the colour of secrets. She swallows the secrets and they disappear but they haven't gone away. They are inside her.

Evil Gifts

THERE WERE a lot of snakes in our lives at this time. At our mother's house enormous carpet pythons wound themselves around the rafters of the verandahs. When Lizzie saw one, she'd capture Artemis and shut her in her room. She'd known someone who'd had a kitten taken by a carpet snake once; Artemis was bigger than that, but Lizzie was taking no chances.

Snakes curled up in dark corners of Emma's studio; they stretched along the noggins of the unlined walls, still and milky eyed, and shed their skins. Her studio was a perfect place for snakes, dim and cool and surrounded by sheltering trees. Only Emma disturbed the stillness, scratching softly at her easel. She and the snakes tolerated each other; I think she quite liked them.

We found snake skins everywhere: wafting from the rafters like pennants or drifting like leaves on the verandah floors. I loved the pattern of three diamonds across the back, the delicacy of the scales, like fine bubble-wrap. The dry skins rustled when you touched them, but sometimes we found one moist and recently vacated. Chloe collected them; she planned to give them all to Paris. She still tried to please her always.

I don't mean the snakes to be symbolic of anything; you can take them any way you like. I mention them because they were there. They were part of the texture of our lives. A fact. A snake can simply be a snake.

∽

Lizzie was good at swallowing things. She swallowed the goblin man's evil gifts and went back for more. I don't know what she did there. Maybe she just cleaned off the dribble of tannin under his teapot spout, or watered the wilting herbs in the garden planted by that Jamila person, or learned to appreciate his badly written poetry at last.

When we were at Claudio's she disappeared for long afternoons at a time. I prowled the streets sometimes looking for her, and one afternoon I spotted her in an outdoor cafe. The goblin man was with her. I watched as he said something to her and slid his finger along the top of her upturned wrist. Without another word he got up and left, as smoothly as a snake. I followed him, not daring to catch up, wondering what I would say to him if I did. Then, as he reached his front gate he turned his head and looked at me, as still as something about to pounce. I took the next few metres in great strides, urgently, and he waited, seeing that I had something to say to him. 'Leave my sister alone,' I blurted out. I was Claudio's daughter as I said it, my brows running together fiercely, my eyes flashing fire.

He laughed, his face full of astonishment and mockery. 'And who might your sister be?'

'Lizzie.'

'Lizzie is *your* sister?'

I nodded, insulted by the disbelief on his face.

'Look, Lizzie is her own person,' he said. 'She does what she wants to do. If you don't know that, then you don't know the first thing about your sister.' His words were slow and soft. I don't remember him doing anything as ordinary as turning and going into the house. The next moment he simply wasn't there.

❧

Claudio loved Stella. His eyes flashed with adoration for her; it was embarrassing. He'd pick her up and hold her above him as if she were a child, laughing and looking up at her, his eyes alive.

Stella was nonchalant about all this adoration; she took it as her due. She stayed out late as she felt like it, and never bothered to ring to say where she was on those nights. He looked after us all, including Paris, on his own, but his face became anxious and then enraged as the evening progressed. There were arguments, which we heard from the shelter of our room.

Paris crept around, keeping to herself. I often saw her inquisitive face before she disappeared through a doorway. At that time Stella wore the long black velvet coat that set off her blonde hair and creamy skin. It must have been winter, for she wore it often. 'My mother's coat,' she'd said carelessly, the first time she put it on, and Claudio cast an admiring glance at her. 'She bought it in Paris. The first time she went there, before she had me. I used to dress up in it when I was a kid.' How Lizzie and I admired and envied that coat, gilded as it was by being part of our mother's Great Aunt Em story. It was a part of our folklore, part of the only story our mother had consented to tell us.

Claudio adored Stella whatever she wore. I'd catch him looking at her and have to turn away.

෨

Our mother couldn't always conceal her pain from us. There's a part of my story that causes me pain to tell.

There was a gathering at which my mother's friend Mishka was to play the trumpet in a jazz band. (Mishka had just turned fifty: she said to my mother, 'Now I'm blowing my own trumpet at last.') Imagine a darkened hall; tables with candles, people everywhere; my mother to one side of the room watching the band warm up; and then,Claudio and Stella arriving at the door. I saw the expression on my mother's face. She looked away.

Claudio registered Emma's presence too. There was surprise – no pain – then it was gone. Claudio was a great concealer. He met up with people, talked and laughed. My father was always the life of the party.

Stella was wearing her mother's coat. She stood there in it, ice-cool, her skin like cream, smiling to herself, staring at the floor. Our mother pushed her way from the room, out a side door, so she wouldn't have to go past them.

Lizzie lay stretched out on her bed and I crept up to her and laid my head on her belly. At fourteen I was still young enough to do that and get away with it. I knew that the shorts I wore and my sturdy brown legs and short cropped curls made me look a child still. It allowed me to do lots of things that more dignified people would think beneath them, but it was also my greatest source of sorrow, that Lizzie and I didn't look more alike.

'Don't go to see that man again,' I begged, aware of how pathetic I was. I couldn't stop myself. 'He looks like an evil fairy.' I sat up and slid my hand under her blouse and felt the smooth skin of her waist. My fingers touched the cool ring embedded in her skin; I slipped the tip of my index finger into the ring for an instant. She pushed me away. 'Oh, Laura, get *off* me.'

'But why do you visit him?' I put my hand on her thigh and she slapped it away.

'Stop touching my *leg*!'

She began to dress with care, pulling a flimsy purple top from a hanger. She unearthed a slim-fitting long magenta skirt from a pile on the floor and shook it out. Her hair she unbraided and brushed so that it stood out in crinkles over her shoulders like a gold cape. I lay on the bed and watched. She coated her lips with mulberry lipstick and then ate most of it off again while she daubed rose geranium oil on her wrists.

I lay on her bed as she left. A sickly sweet trail of scent was all that was left of her. I rolled over and put my nose into her pillow and her bed still smelt of the real Lizzie.

She goes to the goblin man's house, her hair unbraided, dressed like an offering. She walks straight through the front door, a door that is rarely closed, and up the dark stem of hallway to where the house opens out into a cluttered back verandah. The goblin man is not alone.

Stella is there. She is sprawled on the sofa, her head reclining against a cushion. The goblin man is beside her, curled up with his ear against her belly.

He looks up at Lizzie, his one visible eye glittering like a raven's. Lizzie turns without a word and goes out.

'What happened?' I asked her when she returned.

'Nothing. Nothing happened.'

I looked at her, not believing. Yet she had been gone only a short time.

'Truly,' she said. 'Nothing happened. Then, or ever. He never touched me.'

She laughed with relief. She lay on the bed and hugged her knees to her chest.

All that time spent hanging round the goblin man and nothing had happened. Something was going on but nothing had happened.

It wasn't long before she began to ask herself if he was even real.

She asked me to come with her to the hairdresser's where she sat stiffly in front of the mirror, her hair in a single plait that fell behind like a rope. The hairdresser was young, with white hair clipped close to his head and a thin face. He tied a rubber band around the top of the plait and severed it cleanly just above the band. With a war whoop he dropped it into Lizzie's lap. 'Scalped!' he said.

The buzz of conversation in the salon stopped for a moment as everyone turned to look. It was odd, like the world stopping, and then starting up again as if nothing had happened. The place was more like a party than a hairdresser's; it was full of people talking about the kind of music Lizzie and I never listened to.

Lizzie bowed her head and refused to look in the mirror as he got to work on what remained of her hair. When it was finished she raised her eyes; he held a mirror behind her so she could see it from all sides, and I could tell that she liked what she saw.

'Very, very nice,' said the hairdresser with admiration. 'You're a new woman!'

I stared at her shyly. The cut was short and feathery, shaped into the nape of her long, pale neck. She stood up. And again, everyone left off what they were doing or saying for a moment to observe her with long glances of envy.

She put the plait into her bag, went to the counter and paid; I got up to go with her, and it was like attending a queen. We went out into an ordinary Mullumbimby afternoon. I skipped a hop and a step to keep up as she made her way down the street; I saw her catch sight of her reflection in a shop window and admire herself secretly.

We passed an old woman in a purple hat, a hat that you felt you could eat, for it had a bloom on it like a ripe plum, and Lizzie smiled to herself. We walked on, and were halfway down the street before I said, 'You liked that hat.'

'You liked *her* in that hat,' I amended.

She smiled down at me, sideways, a small complicit smile that let me know I was exactly right. She said, 'I enjoy it when old ladies dress up. When *I* am old, I'll wear the most beautiful clothing I can find.'

We passed the op shop and with one accord stopped and went back to it. Lizzie loved the clothes that other women had discarded. She slipped into them eagerly, loving how they transformed her, loving how she transformed them and gave them new life.

'I need a hat,' she said.

We found the perfect hat for Lizzie first off. It was as old as old, made of black velvet with a low crown and no brim, and had an ancient stiff hatpin with a single pearl embedded in the side. It smelt of dust and lavender perfume.

'It's the sort of hat Aunt Em might have worn,' I said.

'Exactly,' she said, her voice round and fat and satisfied, and took the hat straight to the counter. She wore it out of the shop.

When we got home Lizzie didn't remove her hat at once, and I don't think our mother noticed that she'd cut her hair. Then Lizzie reached into her bag and threw the severed plait onto the table.

Stella and Paris arrived in the middle of a storm. Emma had been standing on the verandah enjoying the crash of thunder and the beat of the rain, as she always did – she liked the *tempestuousness* of it – when Stella's old yellow Corona toiled up the drive. Torrents of water poured from the sky and rendered the car almost invisible. Emma watched as Stella climbed out, the door almost wrenched away from her by the wind, and climbed the front steps of the house without bothering to run or hunch her shoulders as people do in the rain, simply allowing herself to get drenched. Her hair was plastered down over her head and her mouth was open.

Emma met her at the front door, took in her condition, and ushered her inside without a word. She left her dripping in the kitchen and took some raingear outside to help Paris out of the car and into the house.

When she was a child, Flora had said that Stella was a star. She was also a drama queen. 'I've left him!' she said, the moment Emma got back. 'God, what a bastard! I wonder that you stuck to him all those years!'

Paris watched with a cynical expression. Lizzie went off to her room. But of course I stayed on to see what happened. Emma calmly found dry clothes, offered food, and made them up a bed each.

‷

Emma could have asked *why* or *how* but she didn't want to know the details. Anyway, who can say what goes on between people where love is concerned?

Only Paris had seen the end of Claudio and Stella's affair. Alone in the house with them, as she often was when we weren't there, she had heard the angry and then resigned words in the bedroom. She heard them go out.

She followed down the windy winter street. Neither glanced back to see the small figure in teacup-printed pyjamas as she padded barefoot down the ill-lit pavement behind them. Stella huddled into her black coat and Claudio shivered in a cotton shirt.

⁂

And Paris sees them enter the darkened silent park, empty of people or lights. She stands at a distance and watches as Stella spreads her coat on the ground under the shelter of some trees, and she and Claudio, on the coat, fuck for the last time.

⁂

On the second day of rain, after we'd finished dinner, Stella and Emma and I sat listening to the calls of frogs from the puddles that had been created around the house. It was an awkward silence; no one spoke. The rhythm of the frog calls beat inside my head. Lizzie had eaten quickly and sparingly and gone to her room.

It had stopped raining, and Chloe and Paris had gone outside. Emma suddenly got to her feet and went to find them. 'Chloe! Paris!'

I followed. They looked up at the dazzling eye of Emma's torch. 'Come and look for frogs with me!'

We followed the call of the frogs, a regular *unk, unk, unk,* our footsteps making the torches bounce. We stopped when the sound was right in front of us. Emma leaned over a puddle and spotlighted a small frog floating on the surface of the water. Paris caught it in a jar, and we took it back to the house to look at it properly. It was a woebegone little frog, small and warty, and with one suckered foot against the wall of the jar. We could see its soft, pale underbelly.

'An ornate burrowing frog,' said Emma, who knew about these things.

'No it's not,' said Paris, 'It's a yukky little toad. The kind a witch might have.'

'No, it's a frog,' said Emma. 'The only toad in Australia is introduced – the cane toad. But this isn't one of them – it's an adult frog, even though it's so small. This one is *Limnodynastes ornatus*. The ornate burrowing frog. *Limnodynastes* means "lord of the marshes". Don't you think he looks like a little lord?'

'I'd hate to kiss him,' said Chloe, wrinkling up her nose, 'even if he really was a handsome prince.'

'*I'd* kiss him,' said Paris. 'And I'd cut him up too. I'd love to cut up a frog.'

'I don't think we'll kiss this one, or cut it up,' said Emma. 'When we've had a bit more of a look we'll put him back in the puddle.'

'You should be wary of kissing frogs,' drawled Stella, her face turned towards them in the darkness, from where she'd been leaning over the edge of the verandah with a cigarette. The tip glowed as she inhaled. 'You never know what kind of prince it might turn into.'

Lizzie's shape appeared in the shadowy doorway for a moment, but when I looked properly she was gone. I think I saw my mother smile. I may have even heard her laugh, a soft chuckle. Stella glanced quickly in her direction and then back out at the night.

❧

Lizzie was careful to avoid Stella; it was easy, for it was a big house, sprawling, made for people to be able to go off on their own. It was the only reason our mother and Stella had been able to live there together for the past week.

Lizzie had worn the velvet hat ever since she'd bought it. I found her late one night, lying on her bed like a corpse, her hands folded on her chest, the hat still on her head.

Without looking at me she said, 'Sometimes I think I'll die from not speaking.'

I crept onto the end of the bed.

'I hate the way she puts up with everything. And allowing *her* back here like that, after what she's done. I just wish I could say it all to them, that's all.'

❧

Because we mostly ignored her, Paris kept to her solitary habits. I'd see her scribbling in her notebook, probably writing down observations of us. She was like an anthropologist studying a strange tribe, only the tribe she was studying was us, *the Zucchinis*.

She kept a collection of moth wings in that notebook. I'd see one fall out when she opened it; see her pick it up and replace it between the pages, wiping the dust from its wings off her fingers.

❧

Paris, ever curious, wonders what the difference is between a moth and a butterfly. Looking in the dictionary she finds that among other things, moths have *nocturnal and crepuscular habits*. She looks up *crepuscular* and writes the word in her notebook.

&

Our mother and Paris had grown to like each other. You could tell from the way they did things together, Paris watching Emma carefully.

Emma allowed Paris to be there while she sketched. She drew a picture of a woman in a dress made of a whole snakeskin, the head and open mouth of the snake forming a hood, so that only the woman's face showed.

'Where are her legs?' whispered Paris.

'Perhaps she doesn't have any,' Emma whispered back.

'Or they're in the tail of the snake.'

Emma drew the dress so that it ended in a tail.

'Did she kill the snake to make her dress?'

'I think maybe she's being eaten by the snake. Consumed by it . . .'

'Consumed . . .' said Paris, liking the sound of the word. 'Why are we whispering?'

'I don't know,' Emma whispered back. 'Maybe we don't want to disturb her. Maybe she *is* the snake. She might bite us.' They laughed silently together, covering their mouths in an exaggerated way with their hands.

'Which is it, though?' insisted Paris. 'Is she being . . . *consumed* . . . by the snake, or is she the snake herself?'

'I don't know,' said Emma. 'Maybe both. All things are possible.'

Paris stroked Emma's hair. 'A lot of your hairs are silver,' she said, picking up a strand and examining it. 'They're beautiful.'

'Yes,' said Emma. 'I'm going grey. I intend to cultivate my hair to the exact shade of grey I like. I want it to have a soft sheen, like pewter.'

They walked the garden together, Paris with the skin of a small diamond python wrapped around her wrist, Emma with her favourite hemp gardening hat almost obscuring her face. Emma named the plants as if reciting a poem: *heartsease and hyssop, borage and bitter root, bittersweet, blackberry, lemon balm and aloe, chamomile, catnip, geranium and henbane, lavender, rosemary . . .*

❧

They squat down to pinch fragrant leaves between their fingers. The snakeskin Paris wears on her wrist rustles against the rosemary bush. Her eyes, dark with knowledge, are level with Emma's.

'We're having a baby,' she says.

She watches until she sees that her words have entered Emma's consciousness. 'I hope I get a sister.'

Emma stands up, her hand on the small of her back, as if it aches. Paris is too old not to know what effect her words might have. And too young to really know what she is doing.

✌

Emma went to Stella and said, 'I think you ought to leave.'

Now that she'd been told she couldn't pretend she didn't know. When Stella had arrived on the night of the storm I said that *Emma took in her condition*. I didn't just mean that Stella was soaking wet and distressed. Emma knew all along she was pregnant, though it didn't show. Some women can scent these things, and my mother is one of them.

✌

Lizzie wore the black velvet hat with the pearl hatpin at the school concert. The hat that we called *Aunt Em's hat*. We half-believed that it was. We didn't have a long velvet coat like Stella's, so the hat served as a kind of family heirloom for us.

Lizzie was in a rock group with three other girls but she stood apart, a bit to the side, as if she didn't really belong with them. Aunt Em's hat made her look exotic and pale and remote. She played her guitar staring straight ahead. In public she never caressed it, or kissed it, or smelt it as she did when she was on her own. And it was only when she was alone that her face and body manifested her feeling for the music when she played. Now she was almost motion-less, except for her fingers, simply a lanky schoolgirl playing a guitar in a desultory way. To anyone else her face would have appeared expressionless. Only I was aware of her secret, suppressed delight.

Kiss the Sky

THE SUMMER when I was seventeen I was so full of un-differentiated sensuality that the world was a great glowing golden fruit around me. I didn't long for love and nor did I need it, yet I saw love everywhere without even looking for it.

'I love you, Mick,' said a girl who'd been busking outside a cafe with her boyfriend; they'd packed up and were walking away with their instruments. She had a round, childish face and stringy hair and her bare feet were so beautiful I could have taken them into my hands and kissed them. 'I love you, Mick,' she said, and her voice was so sweet and innocent and sincere; the words flowed from her mouth spontaneously without passion or inflection. 'I love you too,' said Mick simply, and they caught each other's hands. I saw then how easy and undramatic love could be.

'Why are you looking at me like that?' said a guy at a cafe table as a friend of his, a girl, approached.

'Every time I see you you've got this great grin on your face . . .' she said.

One night outside the hotel at Brunswick Heads I saw a guy and a girl part: you could see they were only friends at that moment but she said, 'I'll see you tomorrow then,' in a way that promised they would soon be much more. I saw the look of delight on his face as he turned away from her to head back into the beer garden. He was so happy he leapt into the air and touched the overhanging branch of a frangipani tree with his hand. Everywhere I looked, there were people delighting in each other.

But I needed no one. I was myself, complete.

At night the summer air breathed onto my face with such promises of bliss that I slept in a deep swoon. I was caressed by the morning sunlight and seduced by the long afternoon shadows, and I lapped it all up in such a daze of sensation that I couldn't tell where the world ended and I began. I was so much in love with simply being alive that I could have kissed the sky.

✌

In the bookshop at Mullumbimby I crouched on the floor, dipping into books. I had a belief that one day I would come across something – in a book, anywhere – that would finally allow the world to make sense, and I was forever alive and alert for it.

The books smelt of age and dust the way only horrible old books can; even the paperbacks were abscessed and flaky like someone with a terrible skin disease. There was an old woman running the shop, and she sat there in a chair behind the counter and a friend sat with her, talking. I let their voices wash over me, paying no attention, my nose rebelling so much at the dust that I was almost about to leave.

'I always wanted what I couldn't have,' said one woman.

I stopped reading to pay attention, my eyes on the book I was holding, but I was all ears.

'I always wanted girls,' she went on. 'I had four boys.'

'Girls can be difficult,' said the other. 'Girls too close to each other in age can be . . .' She paused, searching for a word, and it seemed to take her a hundred years to find it. I think I stopped breathing, in case my breath obscured what she would say next. '. . . catty,' she said. I slammed shut the book I was holding, replaced it, and left the shop.

෨

Lizzie was catty with our mother but never with me. I irritated her often, I knew that, by hanging around her so much and forever touching her and adoring her and secretly wishing I could be her. I annoyed her by incessantly trying on her clothes, even though they never fitted properly. I sniffed them with my eyes shut to try and capture her essence.

Claudio stayed the night once, sleeping in our mother's bed. We only discovered it the next morning when we found him still there. 'I thought you were meant to be separated!' Lizzie said to her scornfully when he had gone, and our mother didn't reply.

Stella had gone back to Sydney after Emma asked her to leave. She'd had her baby and Paris hadn't got the sister that she'd wanted, but a brother. His name was Thomas. *Thomas* I mouthed silently to myself. I imagined his tiny fingers and scrunched-up face, and I wondered if I would ever meet him. But after we heard the news my mother never mentioned him, or Stella, or Paris, again, and I almost forgot he existed.

Lizzie left school. She said she couldn't stand any more study and found a job in a cafe. Soon after that she moved out of home, found another waitressing job and a place to rent in Byron Bay. It was a converted garage behind someone's house. She made a home for herself there with stuff she'd found at op shops. She draped luscious old curtains at the windows and on the walls she hung elegant scarves and shawls. She'd traded in her electric guitar for an acoustic one, and it stood at the side of the room on a special stand, like an important visitor given pride of place.

In the summer holidays after my final year of school I went to stay with her. Lizzie had a car, an old Toyota station wagon which she'd bought for $700, and she allowed me to drive it sometimes. We loved that car, loved its dear little humble shape, its dusty white paint, and the way it putt-putted steadily up the mountains and never let us down.

In the one-roomed home she'd made in the garage we cooked nourishing vegetarian meals and then, unsatisfied, we went out and bought icecream or take-away pizza and gorged ourselves.

Al had gone away to university. Sometimes I found Lizzie in an internet cafe sending him an email. She hunched her shoulders and stared solemnly into the screen, then shot off her message with the push of a button. She went home and scrawled pages and pages to him with a purple pen, drawing pictures all down the margins and over the envelope.

'Is Al coming home for Christmas?' I asked, and she shrugged and looked unhappy. I was with her most of the time but she rarely spoke to me; I longed for her to throw herself down beside me on the bed and take my hand and tell me things. *Speak to me, Lizzie*, I wanted to say, *tell me what you're feeling*, but she didn't. She didn't really talk, not in the way I wanted. I thought that she had acquired our mother's habit of silence. She was aloof, apart, distant.

For something to do we put henna in her hair. She'd let it grow long again and I was in charge of putting the henna through to make sure it was properly distributed. Massaging her scalp, brushing the long strands of hair from her forehead into the thick, foul-smelling paste, was a kind of intimacy. I relished being able to touch her even in this practical way. She sat with a plastic bag over her hair for as long as she could stand and then we rinsed it out.

Her hair turned an astonishing luminous red. I saw her walking down the street, head and shoulders above the throng of backpackers who pulsed along the footpath. She was ethereal, she floated, her red hair loose and flowing like a cape. People stared; some even turned their heads to get a better look. But she noticed no one; she walked oblivious, and the crowds parted for her so that behind her there was a human wake.

Christmas came and went, and as usual we shared our time between our mother's house and our father's. Al didn't come home. His mother no longer spent all her time in bed and Lizzie said that she was joining him in Sydney so they could visit relatives. I could see that Lizzie was disappointed, though she never spoke of it to me. Did the thought of Al, the fact of him, their friendship, which I couldn't fathom, make her happy or not?

I worried about her. She no longer played the tunes of Jimi Hendrix, but she'd been seeing him everywhere. The man in the record shop, she said, was the spitting image of him. I thought she was mad. He had frizzy hair and dark skin but that was the only resemblance I could see. She said he'd come into her cafe one day when I wasn't there – not the man in the record shop, someone else who also looked like Jimi Hendrix. He'd ordered a vegetarian focaccia and a latte. And then she'd seen him surfing, on a board, way out on the waves. 'He was a real good rider,' she said.

That was when I laughed at her. 'The ghost,' I told her, 'of Jimi Hendrix, maybe that's what you've seen. You've seen the ghost of Jimi Hendrix, surfing at Byron Bay.'

I was in the habit of helping her out in the cafe. The owner was a mean bastard who allowed her to play her guitar to entertain customers when there was a break in the work; she was hoping someone would see her and offer her a proper paid gig somewhere else. So I used to go with her and help wait on tables to give her more time to play. Lizzie was writing and playing her own tunes, but she never made up any words to them.

I noticed a woman in the cafe one day just after Christmas. She'd been in there before. I remembered the way her hair was shaved close to her head, emphasising the perfect shape of it, and the tiny moon and stars tattooed on her shoulder. When I took her order I saw that she and the woman she was with were having some sort of silent quarrel. 'Is there any way out into the hills near here apart from in those buses full of backpackers?' she asked me.

'Not unless you have a car.'

I liked the way she grinned back at me, and then later, when I was setting down her food and Lizzie was playing her guitar, she looked towards Lizzie and said admiringly and intimately, so that I thought she was speaking to me: 'She's beautiful.'

'She's my sister,' I said. When she turned to me I waited for her to say '*Your* sister?' surprised, as people always were.

But she looked at me carefully, glancing frankly into my eyes. I was grateful for the way she smiled and said, 'Yes, I can see the resemblance.'

୬ବ

The next time I saw her, she was on the path to the lighthouse, alone, looking out to the splash and foam around Julian Rocks. I came the next day at the same time and she was there again, but she was so intent on gazing out to sea that she didn't notice me. One, two, three times I saw her there before I was courageous enough to speak to her. I was flattered that she remembered me. She said her friend was out there, diving. She said she didn't want to join her, that she was scared of it, of being submerged in all that water.

I almost told her I had an aunt that drowned, I felt such an affinity with her.

Her name, she told me, was Catherine. 'So what are you doing today?' she asked, and I shrugged.

'Nothing. Just hanging about. How much longer are you staying?'

'A couple more days. We have to be back at work after New Year.'

I ignored the *We*. Then I said boldly, 'Why don't you come home with me for the day? I live out there, in the hills. I could borrow my sister's car.'

୬ବ

At my home in the hills, Catherine admired everything: the view, my mother's wild garden, our dark, cavernous house that had always seemed too large and empty after my father went away. There were years of largeness and emptiness behind me that I still hadn't become used to.

Chloe showed Catherine her collections, including all the snake skins that she still saved despite the fact that Paris had moved away. She had wallaby skulls lined along the shelves in her room, and bird skeletons too, hollow-eyed skulls beautiful in their fragility. On her windowsill was her collection of shells, in groups of the same kind, with subtle variations. Seahorses were arrested in elegant curves as though they had died in motion. Along the verandah rail sat all the tiny boxfish that she had brought home from the beach, some of them still with a faint whiff of decay; their skin was stretched like parchment over their boxy frames, their mouths in a pout of disapproving surprise at finding themselves in such an unfamiliar setting.

And along the verandah floor was her collection of cow skulls, some with a line of bullet holes in them. She had stacked them in a pile, diligently. She showed all of this to Catherine with the air of a serious collector; she had about her an aura of self-possession that I envied, as if there were powers in her that were being stored up for a future important enterprise.

She monopolised Catherine, insisting on showing her the microscope she had been given for Christmas. Chloe had already shown me the juice from a potato, which looked like a glistening collection of pearly beads, golden and glowing and magical. A transparent strip from the flesh of an onion had revealed a silvery wall of six-sided cells, stacked together like bricks. One drop of pond water had weed like embroidered pompoms, and slender rods made of a line of square cells glowing like bottle glass against the sun. In pond water I have seen one-celled transparent animals that twist and turn like gymnasts until the heat from the microscope light makes them die.

She showed Catherine the same things, and told her about all of it: that the fine glass-green strands are filamentous algae, that plant cells are rigid with cellulose whereas animal cells are soft and squishy. She showed us both something I hadn't seen before, the stomata in a leaf. These are the cells that allow the tree to breathe. All the beauty of life comes down to this, to these things that you cannot see with the naked eye, and which, when you do see them, are more beautiful than you would ever imagine.

When Chloe finally let us go Catherine looked at me and smiled, as if to say that she, also, was pleased to be alone with me at last.

'She's wonderful. She'll surprise you all one day,' she said, and I felt ashamed of the way Lizzie had been the one for me to the exclusion of everyone else.

'Your mother. She's sad,' said Catherine, after we had eaten lunch with Emma and gone up to my room.

'She's lonely. Now that she's not with my father she gets together with some of her friends and they drink bottles of wine and laugh into the night but she's not really happy.' I didn't want to explain more. That night he'd spent with her was the only one since they'd parted. Now that Stella had gone away he had other girlfriends, all younger than him, and blonde. All looking rather like Lizzie, in fact, but without the thing I can't describe that made her so beautiful.

Already I was planning how I could get Catherine to kiss me. She was standing in my room looking around at all my childish things, her hands in her pockets.

'Come for a walk in the forest,' I said.

It was a way of getting close to her. And I wanted experience . . . sex . . . all the things my classmates boasted about. I was seventeen years old and eager for everything.

A forest is so intricate it takes intimacy with it to know how to look at the maze of plants entwined like serpents: twisted, coiled, sinuous, insinuating. A rainforest is artful and curled and wild. It is the wildness I love most of all. It takes time to know it and love it, to see properly what it is.

There was no path; we meandered where the plants would allow us, and the wait-a-while clutched at us and clasped a toothed tendril across Catherine's bare arm. I disentangled her, and beads of blood sprang to the surface of her skin. I placed my finger on one and put it to my tongue; it tasted salty, of blood and sweat both, not unpleasant.

'You shouldn't do that,' she said.

'What?'

'Put other people's blood in your mouth. Or even touch it, these days. What are you, a vampire?'

I wiped my finger on my shorts.

'How old are you, Laura?'

'Seventeen.' I put out my hand and touched her on the shoulder. I touched her tattoo, the tiny moon and stars.

'I like girls,' I said stupidly. I could see at once that she knew what I was getting at.

'Since when? How long have you known?'

'All my life.' It was the first time I'd said it, even to myself, but I knew it was true, just as I'd known all along that Claudio wasn't Lizzie's father.

'What do you want?' She asked it kindly.

'I want to kiss you.' And then I leaned over and licked the place where she had her tattoo, licked her on the bare shoulder.

'You hardly know me.'

I was stubbornly silent.

'I'm twenty-two. A lot older than you. And I have a girl-friend. Love's not easy Laura, you'll find that out.'

'I don't want love,' I said. At that time it was true. I wanted experience. Anything.

She laughed. 'Maybe not. Not yet. But you will. Sooner or later that's what everyone wants.'

She kissed me anyway, and I was grateful for that. I loved everything about her: her lips, tongue, the taste of her. I discovered that you can love simply the physical fact of someone, every little secret bit of them. I slid my hands down the back of her jeans and felt her hips swell out below her waist. She had two dimples there, and I put my fingers over them and felt how they fitted exactly, as if she was made for me.

❧

Afterwards, above everything, I wanted to tell Lizzie what had happened – it was so strange and wonderful and unexpected. I parked the car out the front and floated on the lightest of feet up the overgrown path to her garage. There was honeysuckle sprawled all over one side of the building; it flopped over the door at the side and made a curtain of flowers. We often left the door open even when we were out, and it was open now.

❧

It happened in the time it takes for a moth to flex its wings: a long, slow moment, a gathering together of potential before flight. I stood with my face full of flowers but they didn't block my vision.

Lizzie and Al lay naked on the bed, their legs intertwined. And Lizzie looked at him with such a wondering tender expression on her face, a look so full of lightness and love that I stopped breathing. With that look on her face she leaned down and gently kissed the inside of his arm.

Kissed him on that pale, defenceless part, the part that seldom sees the light, that is like a fish's belly, or a lizard's: soft, private, vulnerable.

175

Ugly, graceless Al, Axolotl Al, Al who recoiled from his own reflection in the mirror with flailing arms.

She kissed him with a look on her face that I'd never seen before. I'd never seen Lizzie look at me that way, with such intensity and adoration and astonishment.

I stood for a fleeting moment in the doorway with the gold and white of honeysuckle flowers in my face before fleeing, not knowing where I would go. I only knew that I had lost her.

I found myself on the path to the lighthouse. I stopped briefly to put my forehead against the roughness of a tree trunk, waiting for the blood in my head to stop pounding. It didn't, and I almost ran up the rest of the steep path and sat on a seat looking out at the sea. I felt numb, and dead, and sad. I think that had anyone seen my face it would have looked blank. But I had my face turned to the sea and the sky; the murky, treacherous waves and the darkening clouds reflected what was inside me.

I had always thought, from the first, that Lizzie was all mine. I thought that I *was* her. Even after I looked in the mirror at the age of ten and saw that I wasn't I still somehow didn't believe it. But I knew now that she wasn't part of me; we were finally and irrevocably separate.

⁓

When I was a child I was given a kaleidoscope that didn't contain the usual brightly-coloured fragments of glass. This one was made entirely of mirrors, and it made patterns from whatever you looked at.

I was fascinated by it. I aimed it at everything I could find. And having looked minutely at beetles and leaves and pebbles and water, I discovered Lizzie, and I examined her to see what patterns she would make. Her eye became a myriad of eyes, her mouth a carpet of plump pink hills. She was so decorative that I probed almost every part of her that I decently could and exclaimed in wonder. Her hair! Fingernails! Her big toe! I peered through the tube at the intricate mysteries of her curved ear, and I even attempted to look at her nostrils but she pushed me away with an exasperated sound that was the closest she ever got to being angry with me. 'Oh, Laura, just *quit* it!'

When I could stay away no longer, I returned in the dark. Lizzie was alone by then, and I waited for her to speak, to confide in me, but she didn't tell me a thing. We made dinner together and talked, but nothing was said.

That night was New Year's Eve, and everywhere I went I watched for Catherine. The streets were filled with people, music, noise, candle-lit lanterns. Lizzie and I didn't usually drink, but we bought cans of rum and Coke and drank them sitting on the white-painted fence that fronted the beach.

I wondered when Lizzie would tell me about Al, or if she would ever tell me about him. I wondered where he was now, and why he hadn't stayed. But I didn't say anything, and she didn't even notice I wasn't talking. We sat on the fence, and I felt apart from her.

The beach was filled with people walking along the sand, or curled up together waiting for the fireworks to begin. I kept scanning the crowd for Catherine, looking for her beautiful shorn head. Once or twice I thought I saw her – someone who could be her – but it never was.

We sat down on the dry sand, just above the tide line. In front of us stretched the endless sea and sky, and the moon reflected a path on the water like a shimmering yellow road. We didn't speak.

All I could hear was the waves. At midnight, when the first fireworks burst overhead and filled the sky with sparks, Lizzie stood up and walked into the sea.

She made her way out into the waves, never looking back, as if the moon was calling her. Her dress was drenched; she submerged in a wave and came out again, water running through her hair. The sea moved up and down as though breathing. For a moment she stood with the water rocking about her and the moon floating above.

She raised her arms in a gesture of release and lightness, and I thought that she might ascend into the sky and float away.

The Secret History

It is the early 1970s. My mother, Emma (to set the scene, so you can picture her), is leaning out the window of a room she is renting in an old shopfront terrace near the university. She loves this room, though it is small, and the paint is peeling away in broad flakes and the floor has boards that are unpolished and therefore ingrained with dirt and impossible to clean. Not that Emma tries very hard to clean them. Cleaning isn't, and will never be, her strong point.

She loves her small square room with the peeling white paint and the *Free Angela Davis* poster that the previous occupant has left stuck on the wall and which she hasn't bothered to take down. Emma is very much in the mood to simply let things be. She allows biscuits to go soft in their packets but she eats them anyway; she's been known to eat mouldy bread without noticing. In those days she had her mind on higher things.

So, she's leaning out the window with her mind on higher things: namely, how wonderful every moment of life is, how much to be savoured and treasured. To see the distant city skyline she has to lean right out and peer down the brick-walled canyon between the back of her house and the house next door. She loves the sight of the growing outcrop of skyscrapers with a dozen metal cranes nodding on top of them.

If she looks down to the ground and not out to the city she can see her own back path of crumbling uneven bricks leading to the outdoor dunny, and the timber fence that separates her path from the path of the house next door. Beyond the dunny the yard is covered with waist-high grass and a choko vine covers the back fence. Emma leans and leans from her window, sighing with satisfaction, breathing the world in with each breath and sucking up the view with her eyes as if she can't get enough of it.

By the age of twenty my mother had lost everyone close to her. Her father when she was two. Great Aunt Em when she was sixteen. A year later her sister Beth. And then, just two years afterwards — from shock, Emma thought — her mother succumbed to cancer.

Perhaps that was why our mother loved us all so much, why she was always so fearful for our safety. *'Oh, be careful!'* was the cry that followed us everywhere. It was her mantra, her magic spell to ward off the danger and certain death she was sure was always following us.

Emma agreed with the solicitor to sell the family home and put the money in trust for her (it was added to the money from Great Aunt Em's place: a tidy sum), and then found a room to rent in a place near the university. *I am an orphan*, she told herself melodramatically. *An orphan and an heiress*. Making such an image for herself helped her to be strong. It explains her apparent heartlessness. She grieved for her mother; of course she grieved. But she was a girl alone in a big city, an orphan (and an heiress!) and she was determined to make the most of it.

For her first two years at university she had commuted on the train in her pleated wool skirt and hand-knitted jumper, clutching her briefcase. On her mother's advice, she had not enrolled in art school, but was studying for a sensible BA: literature and history and politics.

The first thing she did after her mother died was throw out the pleated wool skirts. She almost threw out the hand-knitted jumpers as well, but prudently kept them at the last moment when she remembered the cold of winter. She bought two more pairs of jeans and two maroon T-shirts, and that was what she wore for the rest of her time at university.

Two other people lived in her new house; they were both men, but they were rarely home, so Emma mostly had the place to herself. The men were socialists; the woman who'd had Emma's room before her had organised women's liberation meetings to be held there, and the meetings continued to be held in the house after she left. The shopfront room and a room immediately behind it were given over to radical activity. Sometimes the place hummed with people, but mostly it was cool and dark and quiet, and Emma moved quietly from her bedroom to the red-painted kitchen downstairs like a ghost.

Her room was uncurtained. In the afternoons the sun flooded in and filled her white room with uninhibited light. As well as the Angela Davis poster, the previous occupant had also left behind a hairy old Greek rug, and Emma sat on this in the afternoons in underpants and singlet and made sketches of people she'd noticed during the day. She sat in a compact way, her knees drawn close to her face, her drawing paper on the floor beside her, or sometimes balanced on her knees.

She collected paper to draw on, of different weights and textures. She even tore the sides off cardboard boxes she found at the supermarket because she liked the thickness and colour and the ridged surface, which changed the nature of the things she drew. Surface was everything, she thought. She liked the way images could be built up on the page, layer upon layer.

So she sat in her room, and the sun warmed her naked

legs, and her nostrils were full of the sharp smell of paper and the sweet, cloying scent of her own skin. She must have been a singular figure, sitting curled in the centre of a grimy wool rug in a small white box of a room in an old house near the centre of the city. She was all alone in the world, but she tried not to think about that: this room was her home, her refuge, her enclosing womb.

Her life was simple. She went to classes. She visited friends. She came home and cooked scrappy meals from a stash of food she kept in a cupboard that smelt of stale bread and sour cheese. To her unassuming mind she was living a life of unrestricted freedom.

There was a child in the house next door, a little girl who played in the passageway at the back. From her window Emma could see her sitting cross-legged with a black kitten on her lap, talking to it. *'No, I said no!'* she scolded the kitten, obviously echoing what someone had said to her. *'You say yes, but I say no!'*

Emma had no view of the house on the other side which shared the wall where the staircase ran. There were children in that house too, and she heard them running up and down the stairs all day, with the lightness of step and of heart that is natural only to children. It lifted her spirits to hear their joyful footsteps, just as it saddened her to watch the child on the other side who played alone with her yes-saying kitten.

✌

One day, when she was sitting at the window at her desk, she glanced up and saw a man in the room opposite. She saw that he was young, and had olive skin and a five o'clock shadow. He was naked from the waist up and had a towel slung over his shoulder. They held each other's eyes for a moment before Emma looked away.

'Hey!' he said, coming to the window and leaning his hands on the sill. 'How are you going?' He had dark eyes; his face was expressive and handsome. Emma's eyes were drawn to the mass of black hairs on his chest.

'I'm all right,' she said, carefully and politely.

The man looked at her appraisingly. 'Looks like we're neighbours. I've just moved in.'

Emma smiled coolly and attempted to ignore him, pretending to work, though that was now impossible.

'You a student?' he called out.

'Yes.'

'What you doing?'

'Writing an essay,' she said stiffly. 'On anarchism,' she added, not wanting to sound too unfriendly.

'Bomb-throwing,' said the man.

'Sort of,' said Emma. She attended to her book and did not look up again, and he went away, whistling.

Emma rooted around in her things and found a damask tablecloth, something of her mother's that she'd kept, and attached it above her window with long drawing pins. She couldn't have an uncurtained window with a man living opposite, especially not a man who seemed inclined to lean on the sill talking if he saw you there at your desk. She pulled back the curtain when she thought he wouldn't be there, and the rest of the time the light of her white room was filtered through the intricately woven ivory-coloured cloth.

Some of the people Emma knew lived in a house at the end of the point, right on the water. It was an old mansion on the verge of being pulled down, and was surrounded by the rubble of houses that had already been demolished. It had an unrestricted view of the bay, a place teeming with the life of industry: factories on the facing foreshore and tugboats and ships loaded with containers on the water. She would sit on the verandah that wrapped round the house, admiring the mechanical nature of it all; she ran her fingers round the edges of the loose tiles on the floor of the verandah and mourned that their beauty would soon be crushed and bull-dozed with the rest of the rubble.

At night the water was festooned with lights, and that was lovely too. Emma couldn't decide which was the nicest place to sit: outside, with the delicious chill of wind off the water and the splendour of the lights, or inside, where everyone sat around a great fire that roared every night in the fireplace in the centre of the living room. The house had been built for people with grand aspirations; the living room was more like a ballroom, but now it was filled with the scrappy furniture that was all that students could muster in the way of home furnishings.

Emma visited at first because she knew a few people in the house vaguely; it was the kind of place where no one asked why you were there. You could just go and hang out and no one asked questions. Emma liked the place, and then she started visiting more often because Claudio lived there.

He was a few years older than Emma and he was from Melbourne; both these things made him immediately more exotic. After an initial degree in anthropology he'd come to Sydney to attend the Film and Television School, where he was studying directing. He told her that he was escaping from his claustrophobic Italian family and made her laugh with disbelief at tales of their excesses of love and anger. She loved his striking Italian looks and his ready laugh; he laughed with her and sometimes at her and she found that kind of undivided attention intoxicating, even though he just as readily gave his attention to other people. Living alone in her white room, Emma needed a little of his warmth. She needed the warmth of that great house and the magic that seemed to envelop it.

Claudio had girlfriends. It seemed he had lots of them, because Emma met different ones all the time. But they were all the same type, virtually interchangeable. The girls Claudio favoured were slender and feminine and had beautiful madonna-like faces, and long fair hair. They wafted (or so it seemed to Emma) into Claudio's bedroom and out again, in and out of the kitchen or bathroom, on delicate bare feet, their long dresses sweeping the ground. If they smiled, which was rarely, it was a smile of such tender gravity that it would break your heart.

Emma wasn't this type. She wore jeans and T-shirts and desert boots sternly and sensibly. She was boyishly hand-some; she couldn't have looked like a madonna if she'd tried.

She had never told anyone at university about her family. She never talked about her mother's death. It might have been better for her if she had told. This was the start of Emma's not saying things, of keeping everything to herself. She knew that if she started to mourn it would become an unstoppable torrent, so she chose the way of stoicism. And stories.

Tell a story, any story, and people will think they have something of you. 'Tell us about yourself, Emma,' said someone one day. So she told Claudio and his friends about the Aubergines, the strange and horrible and wonderful family she had known as a child. She was even so bold as to give their real name; she thought, in such a big city, what did it matter? It was Claudio who began calling them 'the Aubergines', to make them even more absurd, so she called them that too. She had begun to see her early life as some-thing that hadn't really happened to her, and which could be shaped and rearranged into a story to entertain people, to deflect them, even, from the real things that preoccu-pied her.

'Tell us about the Aubergines, Emma,' Claudio would say lazily, lolling in front of the fire, his hand absent-mindedly on the waist, or the breast, of his latest madonna.

And Emma would tell. At first their absurd names were the greatest source of amusement to her listeners, but what had seemed like their strange ways when she was younger seemed tame, now. So she invented things. She had them dressing in Greek robes and dancing in their back yard in the moonlight. She gave their house the black chequered tiles from Aunt Em's, and in her story Mrs Aubergine always wore a long velvet coat (like Flora's) to school open days along with a large red hat (that much was real) and embarrassed her children beyond belief. Emma had read somewhere that the Pre-Raphaelite painter Dante Gabriel Rossetti had kept peacocks in his garden in London, so the Aubergines acquired a pair of peacocks that perched in their frangipani tree and screamed until someone brought them out some bread. In an antique shop near her house she'd seen a collection of small glass spheres containing flowers made of coloured glass (she'd learned the name: *millefiore*, 'a thousand flowers') and in her story the Aubergines had these paperweights lying everywhere and thought nothing of picking one up and hurling it at another family member if they annoyed them. Several windows in their house were broken.

She felt a sense of treachery and shame, telling stories about a family who, after all, had been her friends. They had lived a life that defied the convention of Australian suburbs in the 1960s, eating what was then considered strange food, reading so many books. It was the sort of life that Emma felt might have been hers if her father had lived, for wasn't he eccentric, with his bushwalking gear and love of trees and solitary wanderings?

She could have spoken of the moments of epiphany she'd had at Aunt Em's, but that was one story she didn't share with Claudio and the others round the fire. She kept that one for us.

❧

Sometimes Claudio looked at her speculatively. One day, when she was sitting with him on his verandah, he gave her such a look. 'White socks!' he said, wonderingly. 'I don't know anyone else who wears white socks.'

Emma felt young and absurdly foolish. The white socks were a legacy of her mother's taste but she'd been too lazy and thrifty to throw them out.

'Do you know what?' said Claudio softly. 'You need a boyfriend, Emma.' He often patronised her like this, and she put up with it, because already, though she hadn't admitted it to herself, she loved him too much. When she was with him she felt a sense of rightness, as if they were made of the same stuff. Each time she arrived at his house it was with a breathless feeling of hope that he would be at home.

'But you need to dress up a bit,' he went on. 'Tell you what. Muddy Waters is in town in a couple of weeks – you know who he is?'

Emma shook her head. She was woefully ignorant of things. She'd even stopped listening to pop music on her transistor radio.

'He's an old blues guy from the States. One of the best. Give me some money and I'll get you a ticket. And dress up for it.'

❧

What Emma came up with was a pair of blue velvet trousers that she found at a second-hand shop. They had narrow legs and hugged her slim hips. She found a pair of long black boots in the same shop. She didn't look for a blouse, because secretly, in her heart, though she hadn't yet admitted it to herself (and Emma was good at not admitting things to herself), she knew the blouse that she would wear.

In the bottom of the old chest of drawers in her white room were some things she'd saved from her old home, things she never looked at. The damask tablecloth had come from there. Emma eased the drawer open and slipped her fingers to the very bottom of the drawer and pulled out a bundle of cloth. It was a blouse that had belonged to Beth, and Emma had kept it because she liked it, and because it still smelled of her sister. She took it into the bathroom where there was a scabbed, dull mirror, and without glancing into it she pulled off her maroon T-shirt, and her bra, and slipped on the blouse.

It was utterly transparent. She could see her nipples through the fabric. But they were pretty nipples. She had pretty little breasts. You could see them clearly on either side of the embroidery down the front.

Emma was a modest person. She hadn't wanted the man in the room opposite to be able to see her getting dressed. She hadn't even wanted him to see her sitting at her desk in her private struggle with her essays. But this was different. This was dressing up. She thought that Claudio might like it.

The meetings that were held in Emma's house often made her head spin. People sat around on the bare floor of the shopfront room on cushions or on ancient brown sofas. They ate chocolate and smoked cigarettes and the discussions got very heated. Emma never said much; she was too unsure of what she thought and too intimidated by the people with strong views. The talk was sometimes about politics, about new ways of organising society, about socialism and the Vietnam war. And then there was talk about the politics of housework, and about whether women should wear make-up and shave their legs and under their arms. Emma was safe on the make-up front (she didn't), but she always kept her arms firmly to her sides and her legs resolutely covered by jeans (she did shave).

There was a book that had been published in the United States called *The Dialectic of Sex*, and on the front cover was the warning that *Chapter 6 will change your life!* Several of the women had a copy.

Chapter 6 was about love. It said that people fall in love because of some perceived deficiency in themselves that the other person will supply. It said that people who are happy and involved in their lives didn't fall in love – who ever heard of someone falling in love the week before they went on an overseas trip?

The women related tales to each other of times they'd been in love, men who'd disappointed them, or been out-and-out bastards. At times they rolled about on the floor with laughter, or let tears flow as they relived painful experiences. 'I always fall in love with bastards,' said one girl, not much older than Emma, and Emma felt woefully under-experienced. She kept her mouth firmly shut, but she was all ears. She was still a hopeless romantic. Deep down she believed in the man who would come into her life and fulfil all her dreams. Remember that she was only a few years older than the Emma who'd taken Marx's *Das Kapital* to Aunt Em's and never got around to reading it. She was the Emma who lay in the grass and dreamed about love.

There was a meeting in the front room on the night of the Muddy Waters concert. Emma had no intention of walking past all those curious eyes on her way out.

She dressed quickly, pulling on the velvet trousers (they weren't merely trousers, they were breeches!) and then the boots, tucking the breeches into the top of them. The blouse slipped over her shoulders like a mist; she looked anxiously at the transparency of the fabric. She had no make-up, but she bit her lips and shoved her short dark hair behind her ears. From behind her door she seized a dun-brown duffle coat, pulled it on, and prepared to escape the house.

People had already started to arrive for the meeting. She heard footsteps clattering in the hallway below and the continual banging echo of the front door as it opened and shut. She flew down the stairs and strode, big-booted, down the hall to the kitchen, which had been painted blood red with enamel paint; it flashed past her like a dream of carnage as she skipped down the back steps and along the uneven brick path to the darkness of the backyard.

Beyond the dunny she was safe. With her breeches tucked into her boots, her coat flashing like a cape and the moon flying overhead, she felt in her breathless anticipation like a highwayman or an outlaw. In the back laneway skinny cats scattered. She felt hot from all the rushing and went back to sling the duffle coat over the back fence. On the main road lighted buses ambled past, as transparent as fish tanks. She felt self-conscious as she clambered onto a bus and noticed people either look her way and keep staring, or glance away quickly.

As she looked for Claudio among the crowd of people at the theatre she began to laugh. She used to sneak away from her mother and secretly put on blue jeans and attend women's meetings, and now here she was stealing away from those meetings, ashamed of attempting to look dashing, beautiful, glamorous!

But when she saw Claudio her anticipation was squashed

at once. He was there with one of his wafting madonnas. 'Oh there you are, Emma. Nice boots!'

Well, I don't know what Claudio said, but I imagine my mother swallowing her disappointment (did she really think she'd be going out with him alone?) and trailing behind the pair of them into the theatre, feeling absurd after all.

At the end of the concert, when they were milling about at the entrance deciding how they'd get home, someone touched Emma on the elbow and drew her aside.

'Emma! Emma Montgomery!' It was Blake Yeats Aubergine, her old friend Sappho's brother. Emma had drifted apart from Sappho in their last years of school, and had lost contact with the Aubergines altogether. Now here was Blake Yeats, tall and slender and delicate-looking and impossibly romantic in a cream shirt, a satin waistcoat and soft brown corduroy trousers. They hugged each other spontaneously, and when Emma turned around at last to look for Claudio, he was watching them with an enigmatic expression on his face.

'Look, how about coming for a coffee?' said Blake Yeats Aubergine. 'Now? I've got a friend's car – I could drive you home afterwards.'

So Emma said goodbye to Claudio and walked off on the arm of Blake Yeats, who had always called himself Bill. It was chilly, so he took her to his car and pulled a long black coat from the back seat and gave it to her to wear. It was the coat of a Russian commissar; it had broad lapels and reached right to the ground and Emma marched along the street in it, hands in pockets. In the coffee shop she shook it off over the back of her chair and leaned towards Bill across the table. The dim lighting made his pupils huge. He said, 'You know, in that outfit you look like a beautiful young boy. That's what I thought you were at first, and when you turned round . . . fancy it being you! Emma!' He reached across the table and touched her hand.

By the time he drove her home the women's meeting was well and truly finished and her house was dark and silent, and Emma, who'd never even been kissed by anyone ever, invited Bill inside. They made their way in through the echoey front door and down the hall and up the stairs to her square room with the peeling white walls and the hairy Greek rug and the curtain made of her mother's ivory damask tablecloth. And Emma pulled back the tablecloth so that light could come into the room, and they went to bed, bathed in moonlight.

The next morning Emma got up early, put on a short red kimono, and crept down the gritty stairs and along the dusty hallway to the back door. In the half light the red enamel paint of the walls had only a dull sheen. She went down the back path to the dunny.

The duffle coat she'd thrown over the back fence the night before had been caught and suspended by the strong growth of waist-high kikuyu and lay with arms flung out like a person sprawled face-down. She left it there and crept back inside, switched on the kitchen light and shook Rice Bubbles into a bowl, sprinkling on a lot of sugar and placing her nose to the neck of the bottle before she poured on the milk. In her anticipation the night before she hadn't bothered to eat, and now she perched on a chair and wolfed down the cereal, her legs drawn up under her kimono against the cold.

When she got back to her room Blake Yeats Aubergine was still asleep, the bedclothes pulled up around his neck. He had his arm curled around his head, and Emma wanted to trace with one finger the line of the muscle in his upper arm, hook her little finger into the silver bangle he wore pushed right up there. It was in the shape of a snake swallowing its own tail.

Instead she squatted, knees drawn up again, on the chair at her desk and surveyed her room. It all seemed so much smaller with someone else there in her bed. She didn't feel that she could crawl back in with Blake Yeats, or Bill, as he called himself, so she sat watching him sleep, marvelling at the transparency of the pale skin on his freckled face.

Her clothes from the night before lay where she'd dropped them. Emma reached down and picked up Beth's see-through blouse, putting her face to it automatically. But it no longer smelt of her sister; it didn't even smell of herself. It had a used, unfamiliar odour, of cigarette smoke and her own nervous sweat, a smell Emma didn't particularly identify with herself. It was like anyone else's nervous sweat, sharp and sour.

She folded the blouse neatly, leaned towards the dressing-table, slid open the bottom drawer, and put the shirt into it. She would never wear it again.

The sound of the drawer opening and closing must have woken Bill, for when she turned towards the bed again he was looking at her. 'Emma,' he said. 'What time is it?'

'I don't know,' she said. 'Early.' She wished she wasn't still sitting there in her red kimono, that she'd taken the oppor-tunity of getting dressed while he was still asleep. 'I think I'll have a shower.' She grabbed some clothes and went to the bathroom which was right next to her room. She thought of him lying listening to the roar of the old-fashioned gas heater and the water falling into the enamel tub; it seemed too intimate a sound to allow him to hear.

He was dressed by the time she got back to her room. 'Where's the loo?' he asked. She went down with him, and retrieved the duffle coat from on top of the kikuyu while he peed. When he came out they stood for a moment on the path in the thin sunlight together without looking at each other.

'I can give you Rice Bubbles,' said Emma, leading him into the kitchen nervously. 'I've already had some – or there's some of this bread – it belongs to Lawson – he lives here but he's never home. It's Estonian black bread. It's so dark he says it's like eating chocolate cake with butter . . .'

Bill took the loaf from her and cut a heavy dark slice

from the end of the loaf that was as square and dense as a block of wood. 'This is a quiet house,' he said, 'Do you get lonely here?'

'It's only quiet at the moment,' she said, ignoring his question about loneliness. It was too close to the bone. 'There's a women's group meets here, and sometimes some of them come to work on a magazine they put out. The house is often full of people. Lawson's quiet. He lives in the room up the top at the front – he stays with his girlfriend most of the time, to avoid the women I think. He doesn't seem to have much energy – he eats at Chinese restaurants all the time – he thinks it's the MSG – making him have no energy I mean.'

'What a funny place for you to have found to live,' said Blake Yeats Aubergine, reaching across and stroking her cheek with one finger. 'With all your family gone. You're sad, Emma.'

Emma looked at him for a moment and took a breath. 'The other person who has a room here,' she went on, 'owns a radical bookshop. He's really old – at least forty. He just keeps the room here to store books and magazines in; he sleeps here about once a week – I don't know where he sleeps the rest of the time – the floor of his shop, I think. And he's far from quiet. When he arrives he sort of bursts through the front door like an express train and chuffs his way up the stairs, all fat and unshaven, calling out at the top of his voice, 'We got busted again, Emma! Emma! We got busted again!' and rapping on my door on the way past, no matter what time of night it is. The vice squad is always after him for selling what they call obscene literature. One of the magazines he sells is actually called *Obscenity*. He keeps most of them stored in his room here; that's why he keeps it locked. It's full of *Obscenities*.'

Blake Yeats Aubergine looked down at the table and laughed. The story Emma was telling him was absolutely true. She didn't have to make up a bit of it. But she was aware at the same time of giving it to him as an offering, as conversation, as entertainment, because she had no idea what to say to Blake Yeats Aubergine the morning after going to bed with him.

After he'd eaten the slice of Lawson's black bread and washed it down with a cup of tea, he got up and said, 'I'd better be going.' Emma trailed after him up to her room where he put on the black coat he'd given her to wear the night before. Then he wrapped his arms around her and kissed her on top of the head. Downstairs, in the meeting room, he paused and looked at one of the posters on the wall – a picture of a pregnant man in a sweater with his hand ruefully on his tummy – before stooping to collect several neatly folded notes that someone had pushed through the letter slot in the front door. He handed them to Emma. 'The Henry Lawson notes,' she said. 'Someone pushes a pile of these through the door almost every day.' She picked one up and read it out loud for Blake Yeats's benefit: '*Henry Lawson was born in Grenfell NSW on 17th June, 1867. Henry Lawson died in Abbotsford on 2nd September, 1922*. They always say exactly the same thing. I have no idea who does it.'

Blake Yeats said, 'Can I come to see you again?' and she nodded. After the door had closed behind him the dark house gathered itself around her. Mindful of every step she took, she made her way down the dark hallway to where light shone in through the back door. The bright enamel paint on the kitchen walls made each glossy uneven brick stand out in relief. She flung the Henry Lawson notes on top of the scabby yellow refrigerator with scores of their predecessors and some spilled off onto the floor. They reminded her of autumn leaves, the way they fell and accumulated. Some had fallen open so that they had wings. Thinking of autumn leaves and the dusty wings of dead moths, but purposely not of what had happened the night before, Emma made herself another cup of tea and smothered some of the black bread with honey and sat for a long time in the sun on the back step.

The next day she arrived home and found him sitting in her room. He was at her desk, with a sheaf of her sketches spread out in front of him. 'I hope you don't mind,' he said. 'These were just sitting here. The women downstairs let me in and there seemed nowhere else to wait.

'So you still draw. You're getting good at it, Emma.' He pulled her to him and kissed her.

'We should stay away from the window,' she said quickly. 'There's a man lives right across the way in the next house and he takes too much interest in what I do.' She tugged the tablecloth down from where it had been looped aside.

'You're so modest, Emma. What could he see?'

Emma shrugged, and gathered her sketches together into a pile again, putting them neatly one on top of the other.

'That's an interesting face,' he said, indicating a portrait she'd made of Claudio. 'He likes himself, doesn't he?'

'Yes,' she said, pausing and regarding it carefully. 'My mother would have said, *full of himself.*'

'Full of himself,' repeated Bill, and laughed. 'It's a funny saying, isn't it? As though you could be full of anyone else.'

Claudio had posed for the portrait that Emma had drawn, and it was typical of him: charming, self-conscious, *full of himself.* But there was another drawing of him that she wanted to do, one that she would have to draw from memory, for it would be impossible to get anyone, let alone Claudio, to pose for the expression that she wanted to capture, it was so fleeting.

She'd arrived at his house one day and found him without his shirt. Afterwards, Emma always wondered what was under people's shirts, what they were concealing from others, what the real person was like. It became a metaphor for her.

Claudio was literally without his shirt, for he was in the backyard hanging his washing on the line and had taken his shirt off, probably in order to wash it. The first thing Emma noticed was his chest, which was so darkly and hairily masculine that it set off a memory of Flora's lover, Frank. At first Claudio was unaware that Emma was there, he was so absorbed in his domestic task, a task he was probably not much used to. He had recently broken up with one of his madonnas and, because he thought himself alone, his face had none of the self-conscious self-regard that was characteristic of him. It was utterly private. Pensive, reflective, with a touch of sadness that was accentuated by the downward curve of his nose and the echoing curve of his jaw, it made Emma feel that there was an inner Claudio that only she had seen.

She had glimpsed his private face, his tender face, the face he wore when he thought no one was watching. It was just for an instant, but that was enough for Emma to become entirely and utterly and uselessly enamoured of him.

Emma didn't feel full of herself at all. Much of the time she didn't even feel that she was a solid being, but rather that she was an absence defined by the things that surrounded her, that came up to an Emma-shaped gap in the world and stopped. The footsteps of the children that sounded through the wall formed part of her outline, so too did the voices from the meetings.

When she had the house to herself she was composed of the shadows that curled around her like smoke. She was an outline of shadows. Even when she basked in the sun on the back step or on the hairy rug in the middle of her room, she was simply something that soaked up the sun. This absence of herself wasn't an unpleasant feeling. When she poured tea, it was the streaming of the aromatic liquid into the cup that defined her; when she bathed, it was the roar of the gas jet and the prickle of the water on her skin.

And now here was Bill, whom she couldn't quite believe in. It was hard for her to get used to this new way of being with someone she'd known since childhood. When she lay beside him it was like possessing a part of her childhood that had been most exotic and unattainable to her, and yet he was entirely new to her, too. She was never sure what to call him. It seemed a new name would be necessary for such a new way of seeing him. One thing she'd learned: being close to someone, kissing them, seeing how they loved, made them seem a different person entirely. Even his face was different close up. He seemed to be entirely unrelated to the Aubergine family she'd known when she was younger. He was something uniquely hers.

She liked sleeping with him, the comfort of it, body to body, naked flesh to naked flesh. What most people would call the actual sex part of it was a blur and an embarrassment sometimes, and she didn't like to think of it, it was so unthinkable and new. But skin is sex, breath is sex, and so is whispering. She traced the long curve of his back as he lay sleeping beside her on his stomach; she put out one finger to touch the sandy hairs that sprang from the sideburns on his face. She lay awake and listened to his slow breath in the dark.

&

In the Botanic Gardens they wandered down serpentine paths. Emma loved tangled, moist vegetation, and here there were dank paths surrounded by the swampy green of rush, fungus, moss, leaf frond, petal, shoot and tendril. The stink of it curled into her nostrils. Her spirit plunged into the rank, seething lushness and she swooned and forgot Blake Yeats Aubergine altogether, she was so drenched by it.

They came across a glass pyramid, entered its muggy atmosphere and stood on an elevated walkway gazing out. Their pale faces looked back at them in the glass, and Emma felt herself germinate, sprout, shoot. She felt juicy and alive.

She laughed aloud in her joy, and bent down to a pool of water where a golden carp waved its frond of tail. Her face was there too, and she reached out and dabbled the water into ripples which shimmered for a while before arranging itself into her features again.

When she stood up Blake Yeats took her into his arms and put his mouth near her ear, and his voice was sibilant, like the swoosh of the sea. 'I want to tell you a secret,' he whispered.

She waited a moment without curiosity or anticipation.

'I wish you were a man,' he said.

❧

Within a month he was gone.

She received a postcard when he arrived in London and then a few weeks later another from Amsterdam telling her that he'd decided to stay in Europe indefinitely. Emma stood near the front door in the darkened meeting room with the postcard in her hand. As she stood, uncertain of what she would do next, a pile of folded notes cascaded through the letter slot, slid across the worn lino and came to a halt. Emma seized one and opened it. *Henry Lawson was born . . . Henry Lawson died . . .*

Emma tugged open the front door, stepped outside, and saw an old man making his way down the street. She caught him up, standing in front of him and blocking his way. He wore a white shirt with a grimy collar; instead of a top button there was a safety pin. 'Why do you keep putting those notes through our door?' she demanded.

He blinked behind his round glasses. Emma repeated the question.

'Henry Lawson,' he said, waving his arm towards the posters stuck to the window of the shop in front of the hessian curtain. 'He believed in the same things that you young people do.'

Emma thought that he was absolutely mad. And she decided that she had to forget about Blake Yeats Aubergine once and for all.

She went inside and made a cup of tea. She cleaned the kitchen and put on a load of washing in the old twin-tub washing machine. She swept the darkened staircase and the grimy passageway downstairs, and she went out and bought a bag of oranges and arranged them in a bowl on the kitchen table.

In the weeks that followed her moods changed almost daily. Emma felt that she was waiting for something, but she wasn't sure quite what. There were days when she was so full of lightness and warmth that she felt she might take off and fly, and days on end when she felt heavy and dragged down by gravity and boredom. There were unexpected, blessed days when she strode through the streets flashing with energy and feeling like a young prince. Those days were the best, and at night, when she closed her eyes and slept at last, she dreamed that from the windows of her small white room she could see, not the city, but a glorious countryside of mountains and rivers and great wide plains.

Desires and Consequences

THERE HAD been another train journey, another meeting at a station, another visit, but it was a story our mother never told us until I asked much later. It was perhaps the story that the one about Aunt Em was meant to deflect us from.

It was Flora my mother was going to visit. Flora from Aunt Em's. But she didn't live up north any more; she lived close to Sydney, only a couple of hours away by train.

Flora wore blue overalls that day, and gumboots. Her straight blonde hair no longer reached down to her bottom; it swung around her face in a long bob. She didn't kiss Emma hello. 'I don't believe in kissing,' she said, and Emma was glad. She didn't want to be on kissing terms with Flora.

But they were pleased to see each other, anyway. Flora picked up Emma's bag as if it weighed nothing, carried it to her ute, threw it into the back, and drove home at high speed without a word. She jumped down from the cab, seized Emma's bag and ducked down an overgrown path to the front door.

Her house was in the country, a small cottage with a high pointed roof and a dormer window poking out above trees in a wild garden. A wisp of smoke trailed from the chimney. It was a fairytale cottage. The cottage of a witch from a fairytale.

She pushed the door open with her hip and carried Emma's bag inside and dropped it at the foot of a ladder. 'I'll give you the loft,' she said. 'It's Stella's room, but I've persuaded her to let you have it for a few days. She can sleep on the couch.'

෨

My mother was pregnant.

With everyone in her family dead and no close friends, she had turned to Flora.

Stella was now a young teenager who drifted around for a moment after Emma arrived, and then disappeared. Flora made them a cup of tea and they sat at the table drinking it. Neither of them mentioned Emma's problem just yet. But it was the reason she had come and, unspoken, it hung between them.

Flora got up, opened the door of the wood stove, threw a block of wood onto the embers and went out of the room. 'Just getting a chook for dinner,' she called back over her shoulder.

Emma didn't move. She sat and looked about her. Flora still kept an untidy house. There were cups and jars and half-empty packets all over the table. The living room and the kitchen were part of the one open space, and there were books piled up everywhere on the floor; and the armchairs were draped with clothes. Emma felt desolate. She got up and went out the back door. A little way from the house Flora had a black chook under her arm. She was talking to it tenderly, soothing it, murmuring that it would *be all right, be all right*. Then with a swift practised movement she jerked its neck and broke it.

❧

Later, Emma and Flora sat at the kitchen table and pondered Emma's dilemma. Emma didn't really want to think about it, and would have preferred to ignore her condition, but she knew she must decide something.

The carcass of the chook, dead white, sat between them on a blue plate.

'How far are you along?' asked Flora.

'I don't know,' said Emma. 'Not far.' Flora made pregnancy sound like a journey one had embarked on.

'What are you going to do?'

'I'm not sure,' said Emma. She thought about the choice. About the idea that one could abandon the journey. Pull the emergency cord and hop off.

'It's something only you can decide,' said Flora. 'But stay here for a while while you think about it, if you want to. You're more than welcome.'

Stella skulked in the doorway and listened in to everything Emma and Flora said. She regarded Emma speculatively from beneath fringed lashes heavy with her mother's mascara and turned away with a secret smile.

Flora took a wooden chopping board from where it leaned at the back of the sink, selected an onion from a basket, cut it cleanly in two and began to slice. Sploshing olive oil into a pan, she banged it onto the wood stove and, when it started to smoke, threw in the onion and tossed it about in the sputtering oil. Then she took a metal chopper and started to joint the chook, cleaving it with sharp strokes, banging down on the wooden chopping board.

That was the signal for Emma to leave. She made her way outside. She couldn't stand the smell of frying onions, and the smell of chook would be even worse, though she knew that once it was cooked she'd be able to eat it. These days, she was always hungry.

Emma imagines the exact moment when her baby came into being. It was the moment in the hothouse when she felt so alive that she laughed with the joy of it, the moment when the carp's golden watery tail swept past with a dismissive wave and she broke up the glassy surface of the water with her fingers. Emma has seen tadpoles hatch, seen each comma-shaped embryo wriggle and kick out of the transparent egg, and it is this she thinks of when she imagines the moment of her baby's conception, of its coming into being.

She's lost to the thought of a baby, even though it's also half in her mind that she could have an abortion. To the Emma who doesn't like to think of things, likes to let bread go mouldy, allows biscuits to soften in opened packets, it would be easier to do nothing, and let nature take its course.

∾

At dinner Flora said, 'I'm giving up on chooks – have you noticed there aren't nearly so many now? My father died, left me some money, so Stella and I are going to live in Paris for a while.'

Paris. Flora said it so casually, as if it were merely a trip to the corner shop.

'I lived there before, when I was younger. And my mother's in England, and she's getting on . . .'

Emma realised how little of Flora she knew. Only then did her accent dawn on Emma. It was as clean as mint. 'You're English?' she said.

Flora shrugged. 'I suppose. I've lived out here for a fair while. I don't really think of myself as being anything.'

'Your father – you were close?'

Flora shook her head. 'I never really knew him. My mother left him when I was a baby – she's lived with another woman for most of her life.'

It was dark outside and the kitchen window had become a mirror. Emma watched Stella, who had finished eating, put on a classical record and start dancing, ballet-style, between the fat armchairs in the living room.

Emma had always been a little dazzled by Flora. She seemed to live her life exactly as she wanted. Emma remembered Frank, how beautiful and exotic he was, how desirable, and yet Flora hadn't been in love with him. *Stella and I – we're all right,* she'd said. Now he was long gone, and Flora was off to Paris. Her mother had *lived with another woman* most of her life. She said it as if these choices were easy to make.

Stella stood poised on tiptoes for a long moment and gazed at herself in the window, then dropped her heels to the floor and danced away again. In the glass Emma saw Flora get up from the table and go to Stella. She held out her arms, and Stella at first pulled her body away imperceptibly from her mother (*I'm too old for this!*), and then gave in and joined hands with her. Emma turned to watch them directly and caught an expression of doubt flitting across Stella's face; she saw her laugh reluctantly, enjoying herself against her will, and then finally give herself over wholeheartedly to the dance.

Emma felt self-conscious. The play of feeling between them was like watching two people in love. It was a thread connecting them, a thread that stretched and pulled and almost broke, that went slack and easy and then taut again. Emma watched the reflections in the window. It was like watching the images in a dream.

When they finished dancing Flora came back to the table, panting slightly from the exertion. Stella was once again dancing on her own, and Emma was mesmerised by her faint shape in the glass.

Flora sat for a while without speaking. Then, also watching the thin figure of her daughter in the glass, she said, 'Having a child on your own isn't easy.'

'So why did you . . .'

'I wanted a child. I thought I'd cope. I have.' Flora shrugged. 'But it's probably not for the faint-hearted.'

Emma looked at the pile of chicken bones on her plate. She wondered what sort of heart she had.

'Come on,' said Flora briskly, getting up from the table. 'Washing up, and then bed. I need some time to myself to read. No – don't you do it,' she said, as Emma started gathering the plates together. 'Stella! Come and help wash up! Now!'

Stella reluctantly left off her dancing and drooped her way expressively to the kitchen with lowered eyes.

Emma went to bed and thought of Stella, too tall at thirteen, sullen and uncommunicative and watchful. In Paris she'd weigh Flora down like a stone.

❧

If there are sisters, then one must be bad and the other good. One ugly, the other beautiful. One fair, the other dark. One fallen, the other redeemed. There is always an 'other' when there are sisters. Stories tell it that way. My mother said that when she was a girl she took these stories literally. It wasn't until she was older – much older – that she saw that these dichotomies were really aspects of the same person.

❧

Beth was always the difficult one. She spat out food she didn't like, simply refused to swallow it, so there it was – broccoli or mashed turnip – in a big *splot* at the side of her plate. She talked too loudly, talked with her mouth full, and picked fights with Emma, so that there seemed to be a perpetual festering quarrel between them. She ran away from school so often that the teachers knew at once where to go to look for her. When she was young it was the park at the end of her street; when she was older a certain coffee shop near the school. She didn't head to these places so regularly and predictably because she was stupid. It was simply that she didn't care; getting caught was part of the game. And she was clever, so clever that none of this affected her school results.

When she was older she went out at night without her mother's permission to pop concerts with her friends. She went to the airport and screamed when the Beatles arrived. At one of the concerts she wore a see-through blouse with nothing on underneath – she showed it to Emma the next morning before rolling it into a ball and putting it into her bottom drawer.

She was beautiful. Beauty gives you advantages and Beth took them all. People will put up with more from you if you are beautiful. Countless boys were interested in her. They'd ring her up and she'd casually tell them off and laugh at their bumbling attempts to go out with her. She cared for none of them.

But Emma swallowed everything. She swallowed the idea that girls must be polite and kind and considerate to others.

She finished up her dinner tidily. When her mother was tired, she never moaned that she was bored but played by herself in the garden with her collection of dolls. She kept a pebble as round and as smooth as a lie in her pocket to suck on when she felt lonely.

Every morning their mother brushed out Beth's and Emma's hair and plaited it for school. But Beth was never satisfied. She made her mother pull it out and plait it again and again so that it looked just right, though she could never explain what 'just right' was. One day, as Emma sat meekly at the table with her school ribbons in her hands waiting for her turn, her mother picked up a sharp pair of dressmaking scissors that lay nearby and hacked off Beth's plait, just like that – and threw it down in frustration on the table.

❧

Beth's dark plait drops down in front of Emma – she can hear the plop as it hits the table top. Years later Lizzie's blonde one does the same. Our mother looks as though she's seen a ghost.

❧

Emma woke in the night with the urgent need to pee. She put on her light and made her way as quietly as she could down the ladder from the loft. Yesterday afternoon Flora had showed her the outdoor dunny and said it was better to pee on the grass so they didn't fill it too quickly. There was a torch near the back door in case you needed to go outside at night.

Emma took herself a little way from the house and squatted on the grass. She hadn't given up hope that there might be blood one day, though she hadn't done anything to hasten it. She had vague thoughts of running up and down hills, or of sitting in a hot bath with a bottle of gin. Isn't that what you could do? Or when she got back to Sydney she knew that one of the women who came to the meetings would be able to arrange something for her if she wanted it.

She closed her eyes and rocked backwards and forwards and she told herself: *My name is Emma Montgomery and I have no father or mother or sister or anyone who is close to me in the world. There is only me and the night the stars and the damp grass and the yeasty odour between my legs.*

There is the thing inside me, the small wriggling tadpole thing.

She tried to think of Blake Yeats but she couldn't even call up his face. He had met a man named Hans in Amsterdam and he and Hans were travelling to Venice. That was the last she'd heard of him. His letters were coming less and less often and she knew that one day they would cease altogether as he and Hans rode off into the sunset together. My mother knew what Blake Yeats meant when he whispered harshly in her ear that he *wished she was a man.*

Emma thought of Claudio, of his smile and his startling eyebrows and his air of supreme confidence, and of all his wafting madonnas, and he seemed very far away and unattainable. She wiped away a self-pitying tear and took her head from her knees and looked up at the world. The night was predictably lovely, with clear, bright stars.

ॐ

After Beth died there were reminders of her everywhere. The routines and patterns of their life gaped with her absence. Emma's mother couldn't bear to go into Beth's room, so it was left as it was, the door shut. Emma crept in there sometimes and lay on her sister's bed. She gazed at the posters on her wall, glanced through her magazines, hung her head over the edge of the bed to stare at the dust balls and withered apple cores beneath it. She flicked through Beth's stack of records and opened and shut the lid of her record player. She examined the clothes in her drawers, shaking them out and looking at them wonderingly, then putting them to her nose briefly before folding and replacing them.

She longed to escape the dull routine of her mother's suburban house, which was even more chill and claustrophobic after Beth died. All the fighting had left the house and, Emma saw, any of the life and vibrancy it might have had as well. She wished for some of Beth's anger, she longed for her to flounce once more through the door, to yell at her for dabbing some of her precious perfume along one wrist, to hear her say in her careless voice, *Emma, you are just so square.*

But Emma was a good girl, a good daughter. She finished her last year at school, won a scholarship and enrolled at university. She'd have liked to be able to rent a room in a student house but that was out of the question. She longed for danger and difference; she stood in the dusky night and hugged her arms around herself and felt the thrill and possibilities of life.

Without Beth to compete with there was an opening for her to be the bad girl, the beautiful and bold girl, but she wasn't brave enough for that. She couldn't get out of the habit of doing what her mother wanted (a sensible arts degree, not art school) and wore what her mother chose for her (pleated wool skirts, hand-knitted jumpers, a machine-knitted twinset for best). But she practised little subversions. She'd bought a pair of old jeans at an op shop and each day when she arrived at the university in her pleated wool skirt she headed to the toilet to shuck it off and slip into the jeans. They soon became filthy through weeks of not being washed and she liked them that way. She let her shirt hang out under her jumper, messed up her hair, and that was all that was needed to effect a transformation.

Emma didn't want to do things behind her mother's back. But she didn't want to hurt her either, so she pretended to be the daughter her mother wanted. She thought that what her mother didn't know wouldn't hurt her.

Wearing a pair of old blue jeans was the least of the things Emma kept from her mother. She had also told her that she was staying back at night to use the library when she was really attending women's liberation meetings at an old house near the university, the house she later moved into.

My mother understands disguise and metamorphosis

better than most people. The skins you can slip out of to reveal the person you really are. You can slip into a disguise, too. Put something on.

Or you can change from within, become an amorphous mush and form into something other. It was no accident that she created the sculpture of the leather woman. She was as slippery as a snake, my mother.

ꝏ

When her mother died, it was the real thing.

It wasn't like her father, or Aunt Em, who had appeared to be merely swallowed by the universe, sucked up into a mysterious and grand state of non-being. Her mother's death was the way death was meant to be: painful and drawn-out, a gradual sickening and wasting with time for tears and regrets.

Emma sat with her, wishing she knew what to say. Her mother craved sweet, cold things; Emma bought her tubs of icecream from the hospital shop and spooned it tenderly into her mouth. 'I miss Beth,' her mother said.

At another time she said, 'I was always so *angry* at your father for leaving us like that. Always tramping off into the wilderness . . . going off on that . . . *wild-goose chase* for new plants when he had a wife and daughters dependent on him. I did my best to look after us all. I'm only sorry now that we didn't have more *fun.*'

Every time her mother spoke like that Emma couldn't find a reply. It wasn't that she wanted to remain silent. It was that she was already in the habit of not saying what she felt. For she didn't even know what it was she did feel. She patted her mother's hand. She thought, *I'm too young for this. I don't know how to help people die.* Her mother said softly, looking at her pleadingly, daring Emma to contradict her: 'When I get out of here I don't want to waste another precious moment inside the house. We'll take picnic teas to the park, to the beach.'

Emma agreed with her. She took her mother's hand and said that yes, they would enjoy themselves more; they would do things differently. When her mother got better.

But she never did get out of hospital. She died in the middle of one night when Emma wasn't with her.

❧

Their family life hadn't been all dour. Every year after Christmas when their mother took her annual holidays they went down the coast for a whole month to where a friend of hers lived. It was a small beach town, sleepy and dull, with a general store, a newsagent, a fish and chip shop, a boat-hire place, a pub and a picture theatre.

When Emma and Beth were little they all stayed in the house, crammed into the one bedroom with their mother, but when the girls became teenagers they were allowed to sleep in a wooden cabin out the back while their mother kept the room in the house.

On their last holiday, when they were seventeen and nineteen, Beth had abandoned Emma most of the time. One

day Emma wandered up and down the lonely beach, searching out shells and pocketing them. The wind whipped the
sand into snakes that wriggled along the beach and stung
her legs. She came at last to some dunes near the estuary
and sat there, her knees drawn up, squinting at the glare of
the sea and putting her hands over her ears against the wind.
It seemed she was the only person who'd ventured out that
day. She licked her knee and found it inexplicably salty, as
if she had soaked up the very air of the place.

A border collie ran along the top of the dunes, sniffing
the ground. It appeared to be searching for something. It
kept returning to a certain point, yelping, and then running
off again. Emma wondered whether it was lost, and stood
up to investigate, following it along the beach and climbing
up the dune to where she could hear it barking. She saw
then what had been claiming its attention.

Beth looked up at the same moment that Emma caught
sight of her. She was lying on the sand behind the dunes
with a boy, whom Emma recognised as the boy who worked
at the boat-hire place. Beth's skirt was pulled up, and his
hand was on the back of her leg just below her buttocks.
They both twisted round at being interrupted. 'Get out, Jess!'
he said to the dog. 'Just get out, will you?'

When Beth saw Emma she didn't acknowlege her at all
apart from an involuntary change of expression that was
gone a moment later. She shielded her eyes from the sun
with one hand and looked away again, and Emma, embarrassed, ran down from the top of the dune to the sea, where

she splashed cold water on her face and spilled the shells out of her pockets.

≈

The cabin that Emma and Beth stayed in that summer gave an impression of blackness. The unpainted wood on the outside was black with age, and there were few windows so that inside it was dark even on the sunniest days. Their mother's friend was called Marjorie, and she had decorated the cabin with ancient pictures she'd inherited from her mother. There was one in particular that gave Emma the creeps, a melancholy picture of a woman bending over a baby in a crib, one of those sentimental old-fashioned women with long hair looped up beside her face and a long nose and beseeching eyes.

The cabin was lined only with tar-paper that had come apart in places in long, hairy, tarry strips, and the curtains and bedcover were made of faded patterned fabric. There was just one old double bed in the place, which Emma and Beth shared; Emma often lay awake listening to her sleepless sister sighing and rolling over in the bed.

The boy Emma had seen Beth with that day was called Phillip, and he worked for his father at the boat-hire place. They'd met when Beth and Emma had gone to hire a canoe early on in the holiday when they were still doing a few things together. He was handsome (even Emma could see that) in an indisputable, tall, square-jawed, kind of way. He had a broad chest and muscular arms, and fair, floppy hair that hung over one eye. To Emma he was simply the sum of these things, but Beth obviously saw more. She often went to the boatshed to see him. Emma saw them outside on the jetty, her sister in a short red dress, her legs long and brown, one bare foot stroking the other in delight as she looked up at him and laughed. He took her to the pictures one night, and their mother insisted on meeting him first, and told him not to get Beth home too late. She waited up till Beth got home to make sure.

'Snuggle up behind me,' Beth told Emma that night as they were trying to get to sleep, 'and I'll pretend you're Phillip.' Emma was shocked that her sister wanted to imagine that she was in bed with him, and even worse, that she could pretend that her own sister was a boy, and she rolled as far as she could away from Beth onto the extreme edge of the bed. Beth laughed at her, 'Oh, Emma, can't you see I was joking?' and hugged the spare pillow close to her.

Beth's life became a breathless flurry of anticipation. She encouraged Emma to help in her deliberations on what to wear, allowed her to watch as, pink and damp from a shower, she slipped off her quilted brunch coat and into her clothes, a dab of perfume at the wrist and behind her ears. She did this even if she was going to call in on him at the boatshed.

One of the things she tried on was the transparent blouse she'd worn to the pop concert. Beth put it on without a bra, posing before the mirror with her hands defiantly on her hips, admiring her reflection.

'You'd never dare wear that in a place like this!' said Emma.

'Oh, wouldn't I!' said Beth.

But she took it off and slipped it underneath the other clothes in her drawer.

Her mother refused to allow Beth to go out with Phillip two nights in a row, but Beth went anyway, stealing out of the cabin after the main house was in darkness. After that she sneaked out night after night, and Emma got into the habit of lying awake waiting for her, pretending she was asleep while Beth slipped out of her clothes and into her nightie. Emma, with her nose attuned to her sister's smell, noticed that she smelt different when she came home, that she smelt of herself, but not herself, of something earthy and fishy and undefinable.

One day Beth had been forbidden to go out at all by their mother, who'd caught her coming in late the night before. She must have suspected something and had lain in wait.

And where do you think you've been, young lady?

Can you explain to me exactly what you've been doing?

So you're thinking of becoming that sort of girl, are you?

Their mother's voice continued, cold and quiet and relentless, and Beth murmured indistinct replies. Emma lay in bed and heard it all through the thin walls of the cabin. When Beth finally came inside, she undressed in the dark and lay on the extreme edge of their shared bed and sniffled softly to herself.

In the morning Emma collected her sketchbook and

prepared to go out for the day on her own, as she was used to doing, but Beth, her face still smeared with make-up, looked up in despair and said, 'Oh stay! Keep me company!'

So Emma did.

She watched as Beth cleaned off her face and smoked a cigarette. Emma reached for her crayons and doodled while Beth went out to the bathroom and had a long shower. She came back with her face pink and her skin moist with steam.

When she slipped off her brunch coat and began to dry herself thoroughly, Emma, admiring the curve of her back as she bent over to towel between her toes, said impulsively, 'Let me draw you like that!'

'What? With nothing on?'

'Why not?'

'All right, but I won't pose.' Beth picked up a bottle of red nail varnish from the bedside table and shook it. She plopped down onto the bed and, with her knees drawn up in front of her, started to paint her nails.

Emma pursed her mouth as she drew, concentrating, intent on seeing properly: the curve of her sister's back, her absorbed expression as she dabbed gloss on her nails, the mole beside her mouth, the downy hair on her upper lip, her dark eyebrows furred like the antennae of a moth, her hair as smooth as a sheet of satin, the scar on her upper arm from chickenpox and one the size of a five-cent piece on her knee where she'd fallen over when she was five, her pearly fingernails. All the things that made her Beth and no one else.

Emma thought of how she'd seen Beth lying with Phillip in the sand dunes with his hand over her bum. A frisson of disapproval passed through her. *Cheap.* The word that came unbidden to her mind wasn't hers. It came from years of inculcated social disapproval. She feared for her sister, too. If you *gave in*, which meant giving in to your own desires as much as to anyone else's, you risked *getting caught*. And everyone knew what that meant.

'Do you love him?' she blurted out.

Beth looked startled and then secretive. 'Oh, love . . .' she said, smiling to herself in a superior way that made Emma sorry that she'd asked such a question. They caught each other's eye and Emma was the first to look away. Beth leaned over and placed the bottle of varnish on the table.

Emma felt hot, and heavy. She looked out of the window of the cabin. Masses of dark clouds were building in the sky. And Emma felt her own body susceptible to its own kind of weather. Like the pull of a tide, her belly had the heavy, dragging, almost pleasurable pain that meant she would soon be menstruating.

She and Beth always bled together. Emma enjoyed the quiet drama of it, the seeking out of sanitary pads and tampons, the secretive urgency of it all. It was Beth who had shown her how to use tampons, had told her that *you could* if you were still a virgin, and scorned the tampons that had applicators attached, telling Emma that it was all right to stick your finger *up there*.

Emma concentrated on finishing her picture; her charcoal

scratched over the paper. What did either she or Beth know about love anyway? With their father dead, they had never seen a relationship between a man and a woman at close quarters. 'Do you ever . . .' said Emma.

'What?' Beth pulled a dress over her head and wriggled it down over her bottom.

'You know, wonder about our parents? What it was like between them? Mum never says anything about him. There's just that wedding photo, and that doesn't tell you a thing.'

Beth's eyes sparked with life. Emma had her interest at last.

'I know!' said Beth. 'And there's not even a *letter* that they wrote to each other. Or none that I could find!'

'You've looked?' Emma imagined her sister rooting around among her mother's things and stared at Beth with frank admiration.

'Of course. Why? Haven't you?'

'All I know about him I learned from Aunt Em. He liked plants.'

'Well, we know that,' drawled Beth in a bored way.

'There was a fig tree, when he was a child. He grew all these other plants around it, to make a kind of forest.' But Beth was obviously so uninterested in this that Emma didn't say any more.

'Oh, Aunt Em's place,' groaned Beth. 'I was so *bored* there!'

I wasn't, Emma thought, but didn't say.

Beth had finished dressing. 'Hey,' she said. 'Just because I have to stay in doesn't mean you have to. You could go for a walk.'

Emma wondered why Beth was being so altruistic. Earlier, she'd begged Emma to stay with her.

'You can go past the boatshed and give Phillip a message for me. Tell him I'll meet him tonight, our usual place – Flat Rock. Usual time.' Beth tossed back her hair and gave Emma a flirtatious glance. 'Tell him *I'll* be there anyway.'

Flat Rock was a place where people fished, a shelf of rock near the headland where the waves pounded and sent spray leaping into the air. Emma had seen Beth there one after-noon, alone, standing on the edge of the rock with her eyes closed and her arms held out, catching the spray on her face and on the palms of her hands. So that was where she and Phillip met at night. And now her sister wanted her to be a go-between.

Emma hesitated. She was a mass of contradictions, a sketcher of nude bodies at seventeen, but pure still, ideal-istic, a believer in love, a prude even, who disapproved of *girls like that*.

But at the same time my contradictory mother also craved difference and excitement and change.

So Emma, in the long, hot afternoon, went to the boatshed where Phillip worked. She hobbled across the stony road in front of it and crept meekly inside. It was surprisingly cool, like a cave, with shadows reaching into the heights of the roof cavity where oars and parts of boats lay suspended on wooden supports. She could feel her heart beating. She wiped the sweat from her forehead and pretended to look at the fishing lines and lures and children's buckets and spades that were on sale. She walked up to the counter and saw that Phillip was busy with someone at the other side of the shop.

Emma couldn't imagine daring to speak to him. She retreated outside and stood hesitating in the glare of sunlight, then rushed back in again, feeling foolish. The boatshed seemed even darker now. Phillip had gone down the slipway at the back of the shop and was helping a customer with a boat. Emma stood at the counter and saw them through a square of window that was criss-crossed with rusty wire. The blue of the sky and water was dazzling. When Phillip came back in again she saw his shape dark against the door to the slipway. He walked up to the counter and said, 'Hello . . . it's Emma, isn't it?'

He was outlined against the glare of the window, and Emma could see a fuzz of fine hairs on his face, and on his bare shoulders and arms; he was incandescent. He was so near that Emma could smell his sweat, a smell that she was shocked to find not offensive at all, but overwhelmingly attractive.

'Can I help you?' he asked.

Emma couldn't look into his eyes. She couldn't even see him as a whole person. She saw only a smile, and a chin, and a smooth brown neck. She couldn't speak. Full of shame, she hurried out of the shop.

She went home. She told Beth that she had passed on the message.

That night she lay beside Beth. Both of them pretended

to sleep. They lay side by side but separate in the sticky heat of the summer's night, and each thought her own thoughts. My mother's thoughts veered between anxiety about Beth's reaction when she found out that Emma hadn't passed on her message after all, and a reckless defiance that she *didn't care* about what happened anyway. Perhaps Beth would be so angry with Phillip that she'd never speak to him again and wouldn't even discover Emma's deception.

Beth hauled herself off the bed and opened the door of the cabin to let out some of the heat. 'Maybe it will storm,' she whispered, but Emma pretended she hadn't heard. She hoped faintly that the threat of a storm would prevent Beth going out, but doubted it. Both of them loved storms and wild weather. They thought nothing of going outside in the middle of a storm and getting drenched, despite their mother's warnings about lightning.

Emma lay with her belly still heavy; she felt the pull of the moon and tides. She waited for something to happen. For the storm to break. For blood to flow.

She was aware later of her sister slipping out of bed, dressing quietly and leaving the room like a shadow. She put her hand to the place where Beth had been. It was still warm.

It was a wild night. Thunder and lightning.

Beth did not come home and did not come home.

Emma went to search. It was dark and wild and wet and the few streetlights shimmered through the rain.

At Flat Rock the waves rose and crashed. They ran into the sea in an innocent foamy spill and reared again in fury.

There were no seabirds. No fishermen. Nobody.

My mother listened to the waves. Listened to the wind. The moon and the tides pulled.

Her sister was everywhere and nowhere. She was there in the wind, in the thump and roar of the waves. In the lashing of the rain against my mother's face.

Blood trickled between her legs. It felt like the beginning and ending of everything.

At last she went back to the cabin to see if Beth had come home.

She hadn't. But the room still smelled of her.

That night at Flora's, Emma finally gave in to a voluptuous surrender to grief. She stood in the dark and tears streamed down her face and sobs silently wracked her body. She gave herself up to it, became absorbed in it.

She crouched on the ground, her hands round her knees, and rocked back and forth, reminding herself of who she was, for she felt that at any moment she would lose herself entirely. She repeated to herself over and over:

My name is Emma Montgomery and I have killed my sister and my mother died of grief and I have no one left in the world . . .

She cried and cried and rocked and rocked and lashed herself with guilt and regret, and you'd imagine that with all the turmoil the tadpole-thing inside her that became my sister Lizzie would have been dislodged, but Lizzie hung on tight.

And in the morning, when Emma felt that she'd survived a tempest and had been washed clean and pure by rain, she knew that she would have this baby. There was no choice, had never been a choice, because the tadpole-thing that was Lizzie was the only person she had in the entire world.

Drawn from Memory

AFTER YEARS of skulking and spying and watching, and learning nothing, you wake one New Year's Day (*that* New Year's Day), and on impulse and not wanting to stop yourself because you know what you are about to do, you get up and you kiss your sleeping sister on the inside of her wrist. And you dress, observing all the time the opaqueness of her skin, the sureness of her, her solidity, when there have been times you thought her translucent and insubstantial. So you kiss your sleeping sister and she does not stir, and you grasp the keys of her car and steal out through a door curtained by honeysuckle. Your flight is headlong, through a town littered with the debris of last night's revelry. You see a beautiful wasted girl wandering home with one shoe dangling from her fingers and her head leaning against the shoulder of her beloved, and people who haven't even made it home but have passed out on the grass in front of houses – and you leave the town behind and make for the forest. And your car – your chariot! – flies up the escarpment for once as if drawn by a team of racehorses, and the trees stand massed on either side of the road in silent wonder at your passing.

And you are so single-minded you hear nothing, not the slam of the car door as you alight, or the crunch of your footsteps across gravel, or the clatter of your shoes on the verandah or the slam of the front door as you whisk through the house, which is empty but for a child intent on staring down the tunnel of a microscope. One sweep through the house and you're away, through the bushes at the back and down a path where lantana – a thicket of it – presses in on either side. It is the hedge that surrounds the Sleeping Beauty – you perhaps need a sword to penetrate it, to clear it away so that you can wake her up at last, but as you approach her castle, you see that she has got to it before you; she is standing outside wearing a pair of shorts and wielding a brush-hook, and all around her is a ruin of lantana. She wipes the sweat from her eyes and looks at you.

You ask her to tell you what you have longed to know for years.

In doing so, you are both her inquisitor and her saviour.

❧

'You'd better come inside,' she said, as if she had known all along that this moment would come. She told me the story over one long afternoon while she tidied her studio.

I don't remember what question I asked first, but Lizzie's birth and the real story of Beth's drowning were twined together like a vine that is corded round its neighbour, growing twisted together so that they become one thick rope. It seemed to me that the two stories were threaded together in inextricable and subtle ways.

My mother said, 'I never told anybody that I sent Beth out there to Flat Rock. I allowed my mother to think I knew nothing about it. I didn't want to do her harm, but I did. I killed her.'

It seemed that a great weight had been lifted from her.

She said, 'Sometimes I thought I'd die from not speaking.'

ॐ

For years my mother had been content for the lantana to press in upon her studio. But that morning she had taken to it with a brush-hook, and by the time I found her, had cleared along all one side of the building so that the place had a shorn, naked appearance. She had pulled all the branches into a huge pile, and because nothing will grow under lantana, the ground was dry and bare, littered with the debris of dead leaves and broken twigs.

We went inside, and the story spilled out of her. She cleaned her studio as she spoke, putting away pastels, crayons and brushes, looking at the sketches she kept in folders, reorganising them, throwing some out. She stacked the paintings up against one wall and swept dust from previously hidden corners of the room. As she talked the light advanced and retreated and by the time she had finished, the room was almost dark. She plopped herself down on the stool at her high workbench and said, '. . . it all seems such a long time ago. And when I try to explain to myself how I felt and how I feel there is a gaping hole in my understanding. My mind shies away from it.'

Because I couldn't bear to look at her, I switched on the light and started sifting through some of the drawings she had placed in a folder. Over the years she had sketched us all again and again, most of the time without us knowing, for she preferred to work from memory. She told me that is the way to capture only the essentials, the things that are important.

There was a sketch of Lizzie – I knew it was Lizzie, even though it was only a drawing of her back. I could tell that she was playing the guitar, though her body concealed the instrument.

I recognised myself in another drawing. It was just my head and shoulders and hands, though my features were indistinct. My hands were cupped, as if I was holding something, except my mother hadn't drawn what it was – it could have been nearly anything. I was looking out of the picture, sideways, at the viewer.

And there was Lizzie and me sleeping, when we were children, our feet twined together and my hand reaching out to grasp her hair.

My mother said, 'Beth and I weren't like you and Lizzie. Peas in a pod. Sometimes I thought I'd have to *prise* you apart. But Beth – I don't think I ever even touched her. I wouldn't have dared.

'We just didn't touch each other in our family. None of us. I always knew my mother loved me, but there were never any physical expressions of affection. The closest I got to her was when she was in the kitchen making a pie. She'd roll out the dough, and I was allowed to have the scraps to make something with. She showed me how to pinch round the edges of the pie to make a decorative border. That became my job.

'I never really knew either of them properly. People you live with can be both a mystery and so familiar that they seem a part of you. Maybe that's why you feel you can never see them properly. But Beth had a scent that was specially her. I liked it. Playing blind man's bluff when we were kids was always so pointless. I always knew when it was her.

'If you live with someone,' she went on, 'you can't help a kind of intimacy. There's a presence, a companionship. My sister and I always bled at the same time, in perfect synchronicity.'

I said, 'What did she look like? Are there photos?'

'Somewhere.' My mother's face was sad. 'I put them all away when my mother died.'

She seized a black pastel and reached for a clean pad. 'I'll draw her for you.'

Swiftly, decisively, pausing every now and then to remember, my mother set to work. I refrained from trying to steal a look; there was no sound except for the scratch of pastel over paper. The sound was an irritant, for I felt that it was my own skin being stroked, and I rubbed my arms and squeezed the skin over my elbows.

Always, it seemed, I had been waiting for my mother to finish a drawing so that I could see what she had done. Now she tore the sheet from the pad and handed it to me.

I saw a naked girl, her back a lovely long fluid line, her legs drawn up, her face intent on the task of painting her toenails. How beautiful she was, how full of eager anticipation, how unconcerned that someone was watching her and remembering.

🙠

Chloe came grumbling to the door of the studio where we sat under a single spotlight. She said that we'd been talking *all* afternoon. I grabbed her from behind and covered her neck in kisses, and she only pretended to squirm away from me. She took my hand imperiously. 'Come and look through my microscope,' she said. 'We can do *blood*, if you like!'

She had shown me plenty of other things, but blood was special.

'My *own* blood?' I said. I wanted to see that more than anything.

'If you like.' She added, warningly, 'You'll have to prick your finger.'

She handed me a needle. But every time the needle approached my finger I pulled away. I couldn't bring myself to do it. It wasn't because I feared the pain, for that would be nothing. There was something that wouldn't allow me to knowingly mutilate myself.

Rolling her eyes to the ceiling in exasperation, Chloe took the needle from me. She swung her arm round and round and round to make the blood rush into her hand, then she made me squeeze her wrist while she plunged the needle into her finger with one deft movement.

The blood welled into a tiny bead. She squeezed the drop onto a glass slide, and with another slide spread the blood thinly over the surface.

Blood – the stuff I licked from Catherine's shoulder, that trickles from between our legs each month, the thing that relates me to my sisters and is something all human beings share, is made mostly of red blood cells, concave discs that look to me like red satin pillows with an indentation in the middle where someone has laid her head.

My mother and I were the watchful ones, the ones who looked, and never said a thing. There were some things we simply didn't want to see. Or if we did see, we didn't want to admit it even to ourselves.

Lizzie and I had always imagined Beth floating like a beautiful Ophelia on a flower-strewn sea. We imagined it peaceful, like the image of Great Aunt Em dead in her sleep, hands folded neatly on her chest. But of course for Beth it hadn't been like that.

Now I needed to know something I had always wondered about. That night, having looked at the wonder of blood under a microscope for the first time, I filled my heart with courage, and went to where my mother was often to be found in the evening, standing and looking out in the direction of the sea. I could see that she'd been crying, but this time she didn't try to conceal it. Perhaps that's what she had always been doing, standing alone out here all those years.

I took both her hands in mine so that she couldn't help but face me.

I asked, 'Was Beth ever found?'

I saw that flicker in my mother's eyes. She glanced towards the sea. Then she looked straight at me.

'Yes, there was a body.'

I imagined the rest.

I cried then, too, for Beth, because she was suddenly real to me, not just someone I'd heard a story about. I thought how tangled my feelings were for Lizzie, how confused and jealous I had been when I saw her with Al. I let her walk out into the sea in the dark, just like that. She could have drowned. How easy it is to allow someone to submerge. You take your eye off them, you use words carelessly, and you risk losing them for ever.

❧

When I came to Sydney to start university, my mother came with me, and she took me to all the places she'd told me about. The house where Lizzie was conceived is now an antique shop. She didn't want to go inside. We looked in the window and saw our dark shadows against the glass. I caught hold of her arm. We walked on, and my mother paused again in the street, remembering.

'There used to be a betting shop here. A cattle dog would lie in wait with a soft-drink can and get people to throw it for him to fetch.'

We had coffee in a shopping complex that my mother said was on the site of an old timber yard. 'This place was like a country town, once. Now look at it.'

We finished our coffee and continued on up to the point. Where Claudio's old mansion was is now a collection of townhouses. 'Everything is different,' she said. Except for the water, which still glinted in the sunlight.

꙰

When Emma arrived back from Flora's she had no idea how she would proceed. Her stomach was still flat; she'd stopped having morning sickness. Sometimes she could scarcely believe she was having a baby.

She forgot about it for a while. A coping mechanism, she says. She dwelt in her white room. She sat in the sunlight on the square of carpet and drew. She went back to university and concentrated on finishing her final year.

She resumed her visits to Claudio's house. Sat alone on

his verandah in the sun and looked at the boats on the water. Sat with all the drifting population of the house at night in the old ballroom which was lit by hurricane lanterns now that it was summer. One day, passing her in the kitchen, Claudio said, teasing, 'You're getting fat, Emma.'

'I'm having a baby,' she said. He was the first one she'd told. The first person to notice anything.

'Really,' he said, looking at her with interest. 'Do I know the father?'

Emma shook her head. 'There isn't one.'

He said, 'That's very enterprising of you, Emma.'

He started to pay a lot of attention to her. My mother when she was young was handsome and boyish, not his type, she'd thought. But her condition changed all that. Claudio turned his attention to her. He turned on his charm, which was considerable, using his eyes, his smile, lighting up like a beacon when she entered the room. Once, encountering her in a narrow hallway, he paused and ran a hand over her belly. Emma had noticed how some people had suddenly felt it was all right to touch it, and she felt her personal space encroached upon, but not with Claudio. She welcomed his touch. She couldn't believe her luck. His wafting madonnas couldn't compete with her: Emma was the real thing.

One night the drifting population sat drinking on the verandah, the lights winking in the bay. The air was hot and fragrant and sexy. Emma sipped a glass of red wine and it warmed and inflamed her. She had accepted it but intended not to drink it, for she knew she shouldn't. But she couldn't help herself once it was in her hands. She glanced across at Claudio and his eyes met hers and held them. Emma looked away. She sipped and sipped at the wine till she had swallowed the whole glass. She got to her feet and went out into the yard where a lemon tree full of both fruit and blossom glowed in the moonlight, and she put her face into the tree and inhaled the sharp odour of the leaves, the cloying scent of blossom. *Oh, I love him I love him I love him*, she thought. Her head spun with the drink and the stars and the lights on the water. She felt so drunk with alcohol and with life that she thought she'd faint. She put her hands on her belly to steady herself and felt her baby kick.

Someone touched her on the shoulder. It was Claudio. He led her gently to his room and he put her down on his bed and lay beside her, his head propped on one hand, and stroked her belly. 'You *are* clever, Emma,' he whispered. 'Making this baby all by yourself. Parthenogenesis. Virgin birth.' His words were as steady and as comforting as a heartbeat, though they were so oblique that Emma was confused as to what he was talking about.

My sister Lizzie is a survivor. It can't have been easy being in Emma's body while she went through all that emotion: the grief at remembering her sister's death when she was at Flora's place, and now the excesses of love as her head reeled from alcohol and her heart pounded and she thought *I love him I love him I love him*. Through all Emma's excesses, Lizzie clung on tight. Not grief, nor drink, nor love, was going to deter her from existing.

❧

Remember that Emma had seen Claudio without his shirt. The day she'd encountered him in the yard hanging out his washing when he'd felt himself alone, she saw the look on his face: a look of vulnerability. He'd turned to her with that naked look still intact, just before he turned on the self-consciously charming smile with which he always greeted the world.

Emma felt that she was the only one to have seen his soul so naked like that, and he led her to believe it was true. 'All these women, they think I'm wonderful,' he whispered to her one night, 'but you – you know what I'm really like!'

That was a powerful aphrodisiac.

Claudio never asked her who the father of her baby was, and never wanted to talk about it. So Emma allowed Lizzie's paternity to remain undiscussed and unacknowledged. She moved out of the women's house and in with Claudio. She was happy. She was in love.

'I've got some money,' she told him one day. 'From my inheritance. Do you know what I'd really like to do? Go up north and buy some land. You could make films and I . . .' she searched in her mind for what she really wanted to do, which at this stage was to live for ever and ever in a haze of love with Claudio and have more babies, '. . . I could paint.'

❧

My mother Emma, when she was a girl, dreamed of love, and she got it. She got the days and nights of bliss and the heady, fragrance-filled summers, and two more daughters.

Emma dreamed of love, and she got it. And, finally, she got the moments of sick despair when she went out into the garden at night and rubbed leaves and earth into her face and hair. She stood in the dark street and watched, night after night, the house where we stayed with Claudio and Stella after she was left alone.

But that was later, much later, and she was innocent of all that at the beginning. She wasn't to know that love is a charm of powerful trouble. At that moment, her life was the fragrance of lemon blossom at night and the gleam of lights on the water and Claudio sleeping behind her, his hand on the belly that held her survivor, Lizzie.

Paris

Y ESTERDAY I met Paris for lunch, in our favourite cafe in Newtown. It's become like this for us. We have a *favourite* and a *usual*. Some things have become habitual for us. It is like having another sister.

We've been meeting every week now for about a year; our mothers no longer speak to each other, but I see no reason why we shouldn't. I lived in the city for over a year before I contacted her finally.

I don't know why I sought her out. From a longing, perhaps, for a sense of connection with someone in this city that I still feel is alien to me, or a reconciliation with my past. I had started to dream that I was in our house on the hill with the sounds of the forest outside and the ocean in the distance. And Paris had been there. She knows what it is like.

The first time we met, I approached her warily. I remembered that I hadn't liked her. But she was seventeen by then. I recognised her as soon as I saw her. Her hair was sooty and short and furred like a kitten's, her body as lean as a boy's in narrow black trousers and black top. She sat waiting calmly and unselfconsciously, and her pale, clear skin seemed to enclose her core of cool self-sufficiency so beautifully that men and women alike were attracted to her. Many stared frankly as they went past or turned to look back but she ignored them all.

I stopped in front of her table and she looked up.

'*Laura! Laura Zucchini!*' she said, and laughed behind her hand, ostentatiously. For a fleeting, dismayed moment I remembered the way she had watched us all, and imagined her amusing people by telling them stories about this weird family, called the Zucchinis. I almost walked out, but I took a breath and sat down.

I have found that she is no longer prickly and spiky. She often talks about *laughing her head off* at things. She talks to me with serious, unselfconscious absorption in what she is saying, thinking things through as she speaks. I wonder sometimes how that watchful child has become this warm, wise young woman.

On that first day we talked for a while and then she said, 'Come home with me and meet our little brother, Tom. He's almost five now. Imagine.'

Her house wasn't far. We left the traffic and the self-conscious cool of King Street and she ducked down a laneway where some of the small terraces were still unrenovated. Naturally, the paint would be peeling on a house that Stella and Paris lived in. Inside it was full of the clutter of a life lived hectically and casually.

Stella was at home, but about to go out. She was unsurprised to see me; there were none of the exclamations of *Oh it's been such a long time* or *Haven't you grown up?* that most adults would indulge in. She simply said, 'Oh hello, Laura,' as if she'd seen me only yesterday, absently putting on an earring and poking her feet into a pair of stilettos. She hadn't changed a bit. She still had the same childish and unblemished face that no amount of difficult living would ever scar. She was out the door before I could say anything more than hello. '*Not sure when I'll be back!*' she called out and the door slammed.

Tom came running down the stairs. 'Paris, can we have pizza for dinner?'

Paris caught him up and smothered him in the kind of kisses I used to give Chloe. 'No, I think I'll eat you instead!' she told him before swinging him to the floor again.

He looked at me, his thumb in his mouth. 'Are you my sister?' he asked. 'Paris said that one of my other sisters was coming to visit us.'

'Yes,' I told him. 'I'm your sister. My name's Laura.'

His eyes were unwavering. 'I have *fowsands* and *fowsands* of sisters,' he said.

'No you don't, you dope,' said Paris. 'You have four. Just four.' She counted them off on his fingers. 'There's me, and Laura, and Chloe, and Lizzie. You haven't met Chloe and Lizzie yet.'

Tom continued to look at me with a friendly but uncertain expression on his face. I looked back. It was strange, seeing him like that. I had known, of course, that Stella had had her baby, a boy, but I'd never imagined the child as a real person, as looking like anyone, or having a real existence in the world. Now here was this perfectly ordinary little boy, a little unsure of himself with me. He looked a lot like Claudio, and because of that, he looked a lot like me. It was almost like seeing myself when I was young, only as a boy.

Then he did a surprising thing. Without a word, and with his thumb in his mouth, he stepped towards me and hugged me quickly, laying his head briefly against my hip. He patted me with his free hand, and I can still feel how small and trusting and loving it was.

ॐ

Yesterday when I saw her, Paris asked, 'What was I like when I was a kid?' and I answered, 'Horrible!' without needing to think about it at all. She laughed her head off for a little while and then she said, 'You're different, Laura. I mean, different from the last time I saw you.'

I looked at her, wondering if I should tell her.

I longed to tell her, *I'm in love*, but I wanted to save it up. I wanted Lizzie to be the first to hear, from my own lips.

Instead I said, 'Do you believe in love?'

Paris narrowed her eyes, considering. She didn't reply, but after a moment she got to her feet. She said, 'I have to get home to Tom. Mum's going out soon. Come with me and I'll cook you dinner.'

At the back of their tiny terrace, Paris has made a garden. She has surrounded the original square of concrete in the middle with greenery. There is a slender bay tree in a pot in one corner, and elsewhere a tangle of ferns and climbing plants is kept separate from an orderly collection of herbs: great masses of mossy parsley, and delicate thyme and a profusion of rocket partly going to seed. Herbs are weeds, she says, it takes no effort to grow them. But after she'd fed Tom an early meal and settled him down with some textas and paper, she spent ages out there watering and weeding and picking, putting what she collected into a shallow cane basket. I sat on the edge of a raised garden bed and watched. She is small, with narrow shoulders, and was dressed plainly in a black pinafore with purple stockings and the square black school shoes she still likes to wear. From behind she looked like a wise old woman.

I have forgiven Paris her *Laura Zucchini* remark; I've told her everything I know about our family, and she has told me about hers. We have shared stories, and if I have made up some of the detail to embellish things a little, well, I'm certain she has done the same.

We stayed in the garden till it was dusk, 'moth time', as Paris calls it. She says she loves crepuscular light. I think that perhaps she loves the word itself as much. It's the time when, at home, up north, the first bats would be detaching themselves from the trees and flying out in search of food, the black curves of their wings making moving patterns against the setting sun.

It was in that in-between hour, the time when magic is most likely to take place, when confidences beg to be shared, that Paris looked at me cannily and replied to the question I'd asked that afternoon.

'I've never been in love,' she said. 'And I don't think I ever will be – not in that hopeless crazy way people long for. People in love imagine that they *know* the other person. Sometimes they even seem to think that they *are* the other person, or part of them – the other half. But I want to be only myself. Independent.'

Paris has told me that in her family the men are irrelevant. Her grandmother Flora barely knew her father, though he left her the money that allowed her to go and live near Paris, a place she loves. Flora is vague about Stella's paternity. And Paris only knows that her father was someone Stella knew briefly in France when she was a teenager. She doesn't seem to care.

'I think that love's just a myth. An illusion,' she said.

And with that she went inside, out of the crepuscular light and into the harsh glow of the kitchen. She burrowed into the cupboard under the stairs and, like the witch that she has always wanted to be, emerged with a handful of fungi from her mushroom farm, which she stewed gently in butter and served to me with a delicate herb omelette and a rocket salad.

❧

And yet despite herself, Paris loves. She loves Tom as if it was she who gave birth to him and not Stella. I have seen her wrap him in a towel after giving him a bath and caress the top of his head with her cheek, her face empty with bliss. I have seen the games she plays with him, chasing him up and down the stairs of their small terrace till they are both in a lather of excitement and need to lie together on the floor to calm down, her hand resting just where his heart is.

The Good Fairies

I HAD not admitted it to myself, but I had developed my own in-built Catherine-sensor; I had an unconscious habit of scanning any passers-by to see if she was among them. After kissing her in the forest that day, for years I believed that I would find her again. And my patience paid off. One day I saw her, browsing in a bookshop down the road from where Lizzie was conceived. I don't live in that part of Sydney, but I go there often, for nostalgic reasons.

I would have recognised her anywhere. There are people who by their very existence pull you towards them, you have such affinity.

She had her nose in a novel. Her hair was no longer

shaved close to her head; it was in a short bob, jet-black, and tucked behind her ears. I could see her only in profile, but I went up to her at once. 'Catherine.'

She looked up. I could see that she recognised me, but she struggled for a moment with my name. I almost supplied it, before she came out with, 'Laura! What are you doing here?'

In the coffee shop where we went to talk, she told me she was a librarian at a university library, though not the same university I attend. I imagined her wandering among the stacks of books; libraries immediately became my favourite places. I was giddy with love for her. I talked her senseless; I smiled, looking into her eyes all the time, conscious that I was using Claudio's tactics, keeping her attention on me, not letting up, not letting her go. After the coffee, we continued walking up the road, with me talking, till we came to the park on the corner and she said, 'Look, Laura, I'm not going to run away from you. Will you please just shut up for a moment?'

We had come to a fig tree, a sad, city fig surrounded by concrete paths and closely mown grass, a tree that dreamed of rainforests. I shut up and leaned against it.

In the past couple of years there had been a lot of girls in my life. I was always searching for someone. But I only ever saw a girl a few times before I lost interest in her. None of them belonged with me. Being with them was too soft, too tentative, too pale. There was no passion between us. Once, after a party, I woke in a strange bed and saw a girl beside me who reminded me alarmingly of Lizzie, and I stole away before she woke and never saw her again.

But there's a spark in someone that you recognise, that answers yours.

I leaned across to Catherine and grasped her hair at the back. I pulled her slowly towards me and breathed her in. I was full of the scent of her. I tasted the nape of her neck, grazed it with my teeth; I foraged on the whorls of hair below her hairline.

I bit.

She wrenched my hand away and immobilised it, grasping both my hands in front of us, holding me at bay. I pressed forward and she offered only token resistance. Now her lips were fair game, and I explored the shape of them with my teeth until her tongue intervened, and it was a tongue you could wrestle with, spar with, a tongue you could please, but not too easily.

'Gentle!' she whispered.

Her face in my hands.

My own breath loud in my ears. We pulled back at the same time.

An old man sat on a seat with his elbows on his knees, smoking a cigarette, a bored expression on his face. He'd seen it all before. A tide of pigeons milled nearby on the grass.

Catherine said, 'I live three blocks from here.'

&

I remembered that day we met in the cafe and Catherine said, of Lizzie, *She's beautiful*, and then, when I said Lizzie was my sister, she said, 'I can see the resemblance.'

I think that anyone who knows us can tell we are sisters, despite our apparent differences. But now I know we *are* separate people. And I've grown to like my compact, firm little body, my frizz of dark hair, my small nose that curves downwards and that I like to think somehow complements my pointed chin and delicate face. When I look into the mirror I know that I am not Lizzie, but I, too, am beautiful.

❧

And I often think of the night that Lizzie walked into the sea.

I thought at first that she would come to no harm, she was filled with such lightness and buoyancy. I thought that somehow the moon would keep her afloat. But then she waded out until the water had swallowed her, and part of me remembered my mother's sister who had drowned. I stood up, my heart pounding, but I was still unable to act. Fireworks exploded overhead and lanterns bobbed along the beach. I thought she was gone. Drowned. I felt numb, but still I watched.

Then, like a miracle, after her head had disappeared from sight, after the moment when I might still have saved her was lost, I saw her reappear. When we were children she would do that. Hide and then return.

She came out, water streaming from her hair and over her breasts. She walked up to me and without a word we sat down. I could feel the warmth of her next to me. She sat, her feet planted firmly on the sand, her arms propped up on her knees, and both of us looked out to sea at the moon making a shining path on the water. It was like a golden path that you could walk out on, and it would lead somewhere. But Lizzie had come back.

Then she started to sing, as I had not heard her sing since that night when I was thirteen and I heard her outside in the moonlight *raising her voice in song*. It had been one of my miracles. I thought I had dreamed it then, and I thought I was dreaming now. She sat beside me, staring out to sea, singing without words in a voice that seemed to come so naturally from inside her that she didn't even need to try. She finished singing, and then she laughed and stood up, and I saw her before me, her body dark against the sky. She seemed immense, her legs wide apart like a colossus straddling the entrance of an ancient harbour. She put out her hand and pulled me to my feet, and we stood together with her breath against my forehead, and now my mind was full of what had happened with Catherine in the forest. I thought of how once I had been in love with the world – the earth, the sky – everything. But the sky was no longer enough for me. I wanted a person to delight myself in, like everyone else. Like Lizzie and Al.

We went back to Lizzie's garage; she had a hot shower and put on the kimono that our mother had given her for

Christmas. It was old, of white satin with red and gold peonies all over it.

Lizzie took one of my hands in hers and examined each of my fingers in turn, caressing them with her own, before she said, 'Al arrived home unexpectedly yesterday and came to see me.'

'I know,' I told her. 'I saw you.'

She nodded. 'I told him I wanted to spend New Year with you. I didn't know what to think of it all, really. I couldn't tell you at first. I needed to think about it, absorb it into myself.'

I said, 'Tonight when you went out into the sea I thought at first that you would be pulled up into the sky by the moon. And then you disappeared. I thought you had drowned, and I did nothing to stop you. I could have allowed you to die.'

'Oh, Laura,' she said. 'You're always so fanciful. Pulled up into the sky by the moon! And anyway, I didn't drown.' Lizzie pointed out that I didn't need to save her. She says that in some hidden part of myself I must have known that. I must have known that she was on some private, solitary task, and that once she'd accomplished it she would return.

And what *had* she been doing, walking out into the waves like that? (I decided to ask; I thought nothing could ever be gained from not asking. There had been enough *not asking* in our family to last for several whole lifetimes.)

'Maybe it was an impulse,' she said. 'A New Year thing. And the moon was so lovely I think maybe it did pull me out into the water.

'But it was mainly because of Al. I was so happy. Laura, you have no idea. He is one of the loveliest people I have ever met. I've been secretly miserable for years – wondering who my father really is, fighting with Claudio, watching Mum's grief. And now I realise that none of that matters. I decided that enough is enough. I think I wanted to wash myself clean of my misery.'

❧

I made hot chocolate and we lay together on Lizzie's bed. Lizzie said, 'Do you remember the story of Aunt Em?'

Of course I did, and she knew it. The 'Do you remember' question was simply a ritual, an opening for us to relate the story to each other, the story our mother had told us again and again as if it was enough, and told us everything about her we needed to know.

Family stories are like folk tales, told for comfort and out of a sense of shared history, told to bond teller and listener together, and that night Lizzie and I took it in turns to be both. We told the story as it came to us, out of sequence, embellishing our favourite parts with details we either remembered or invented, so we couldn't tell which was which. Was it a red kimono Flora wore in bed that day Emma sketched her? Or white like Lizzie's? Did she possess a kimono at all? It didn't matter, we gave her one. Was Aunt Em's favourite chair on the verandah made of canvas or of cane? For us, it has solidified into cane, and she had painted it orange. Did they go to the beach with

Flora just once, or twice, or many times? Once will suffice, for story's sake.

Once upon a time I thought that the story of Aunt Em was like the story of the Aubergines, it concealed more than it told. But now that I know the way of stories I am aware that secrets are difficult to keep. Stories tell things obliquely.

Now I can see that the story of Aunt Em told it all, and it was prescient that our mother would eventually tell us everything.

It told us that when she was young, our mother was obsessed by the idea of love and yet ignorant of it. She was so overwhelmed and attracted by the proximity of a man who belonged to someone else that she was unable to speak to him.

It is a story about death. A sister who died, long ago. And there is always the knowledge of that sister; her things are thought to be kept upstairs in a locked room that no one ever enters. Better to live downstairs, pretend the things hidden up above don't exist.

And in the end, there is no locked room after all. The window is opened so the air can flow through.

❧

I said, 'Lizzie, I kissed someone yesterday. For the first time. A real, proper kiss.'

She hugged me. 'That's nice, Laura. That's really nice. Are you going to tell me her name?'

'How did you know it was a she?'

'I don't know. I've always known. It's the way you *are,* isn't it?'

'Her name is Catherine. I don't know if I'll ever see her again. She's here on holidays. She already has a girlfriend.'

I hugged my knees to my chest. I was so full of that kiss, at that moment I didn't care.

❧

I will make a grand tour of my family, to tell them about Catherine.

Chloe is fourteen now. She says she will be a scientist, and she has her own way of looking at things. As well as her microscope, she has something which, instead of looking into the structure of things, enlarges them so you can see their surfaces closely. Through this, the leg of a cockroach is a lethal-looking forest of spikes, and the wing of a butterfly is a tapestry that a patient embroiderer with a talent for subtle colour has painstakingly picked out with small, even stitches. She does experiments; she has things growing in the fish pond to mop up excessive nutrients; she has notebooks full of observations and ideas for things that need examining. I like the way she has grown up so suddenly and surprisingly, so that she is herself a kind of *fait accompli.*

I will see Chloe, and I will see my father, who still lives by himself despite all the women who drift through his life. I have seen him with a pensive expression on his face, looking wistful and vulnerable and alone. 'Without his shirt', the way my mother has described. And can't help liking him, because, after all, he *is* my father.

My mother, Emma, says that sometimes she felt like a sleepwalker in her own life; there were times when she was so consumed by grief and guilt that her life was lived through a veil of sadness. She had moments of enlightenment and long years of forgetfulness. She said that sometimes her past didn't bear thinking about. Sometimes, she says, in order to keep a secret you even have to keep it from yourself.

But now there is someone she's been seeing for a while, a man who teaches computing at the school where she works part-time, teaching children to draw. I have not met him but he is kind and nice and ordinary, she says. She told me she was reluctant to go to bed with him at first, feeling ashamed of her humble, aging body and the silver marks that bearing the three of us have made on her belly. But he also is old and not perfect. When he was young he tattooed the words LOVE and HATE with a school pen and blue ink over the knuckles of each hand. They have remained, a reminder of a youth spent living on the streets. When they first undressed each other he ran one calloused finger over her skin that she says is turning to crepe and said, 'See, we are real.'

When I am with Catherine I wonder sometimes if *we* are real. We could be just characters in a story. A story with lives as intertwined as the vines in the rainforest where we first kissed. Where the wait-a-while catches your skin and beads it with blood to be licked away by a lover. Perhaps we are characters in a never-ending story dreamed by Paris, who spins out our fate each night as she unwinds our story from her mind. A story with characters like those in a fairy-tale, where all the women, young and old, are aspects of the same person.

But I choose to believe we are real.

How could we not be? Every one of my senses tells me we are. The scent of her skin. Her breath on my cheek. The taste of her mouth. Her eyes up close to mine, like looking into a mirror.

The dimples in the small of her back, like two thumbprints pressed by a potter into soft clay to show marks of a human making.

&

Lizzie has removed the ring from her bellybutton, and all that remains is a tiny scar. She says we are all scarred, one way or another, and that she no longer has anything to hide, nothing under her shirt. I think she is mistaken. She knows the story of her conception now and has let it lie, but I think that one day she will look up this Blake Yeats Aubergine, and I can't help worrying about how that will affect her. But I know now that Lizzie is a survivor, and it was never up to me to save or redeem her.

But for now I will make a grand tour of my family and first of all I will go to see Lizzie, because she is the one I want to tell about Catherine most of all. She lives in Brisbane now, with Al. They have a baby, and live in a peeling timber cottage perched on a hillside with a mango tree shading the back verandah. Bella, she says, is her little moon-child, plump and round and happy. She makes the most of her. *They are babies for such a short time.*

My mother said that, when she saw the photos of Aunt Em with her mother and then came across Flora and Stella playing in the creek, she'd thought, *nothing lasts.* Now she thinks it does. All that mother-love gets taken up by the ether; it stays around; it accumulates.

When Bella was born I hurried up there to see her, and Lizzie and I stood leaning over the crib watching the expressions play across her face as she slept. We were like good fairies, wanting to bestow gifts upon her.

'I'm going to tell her all the family stories – every last little thing,' said Lizzie. 'All the bad and the good.'

'Don't tell her too much all at once,' I said. 'There's a proper time to tell things, don't you think? And sometimes people *need* their secrets.'

Lizzie looked at me speculatively, then returned to contemplating the perfection of her child.

'She will have so many stories they will be *oozing* out of her,' said Lizzie. 'She will *bore* her friends with them, but they will be secretly jealous. They will say, *How come your family has so many stories?*'

'And *she* will say, *How come your family doesn't?*'

౭

When Bella is asleep, Lizzie washes out the nappies and runs barefoot down the back steps, making the treads shudder, out to the back yard where she pegs the washing unevenly on the line and stands with her hands on her hips looking at the moon floating in the blue daytime sky. Al comes home from his job tutoring at the university and she leaves Bella with him, and goes off to singing lessons, her feet flying over the footpath, sandals flapping.

I can see Al now through Lizzie's eyes: that he is tender, and thoughtful, and loyal. She says he was never Axolotl Al to her, that he was always beautiful, that she must always have loved him. I can see the beauty of his pale skin and freckles and the dreamy way he lies on the floor with his books, Bella tucked tenderly into the crook of his arm.

When I go to see her, Lizzie and Al and I will take Bella in her pram for a walk, very late, through the dark streets, the tarred roads still breathing out daytime heat. There will be roses leaning out over the footpath, and Lizzie will pull them to herself and drink in their scent. She will tell me how she remembers our night walks through Mullumbimby, our exhilaration, and all the sadness we bore. She will say that she is happier now. Life, she will tell me, is meant to be like this.

JOANNE HORNIMAN was born in Murwillumbah, northern New South Wales, in 1951 and grew up in a huge old general store which her parents owned. Her brother and sister were teenagers by the time she was five. 'Our family told lots of stories, many of them about their life before I was born, and I often felt left out. I think I became a writer to show them that I had stories that they didn't know.' She has worked as a teacher of adult literacy, and has written several books for children and teenagers.

Joanne and her partner live in a place they built themselves near Lismore. Their property is a haven for wildlife, as they have a creek, lots of shelter and natural food, and no dogs or cats. 'Tiny bats live in the walls of the house, goannas wander about, and in the evening you might see platypus in the creek, a rufous night-heron fishing, or flying foxes dipping into the water. It's no wonder that the place I live in often gets into my writing.'